The Ring
of
Twelve

David W. Drescher

CHAPTER ONE

OSTERMAN'S RANCH
1900 Hours
20 December

The helicopter hugged the terrain, masking its presence behind the California desert hills. John Mack sat in the doorway of the chopper, perched like a hawk waiting for its prey to come into range. His heartbeat kept pace with the pounding of the rotor blades. He tried to ignore the constant pitching and rolling as the chopper got closer and closer to the landing zone. Mack felt a tap on his shoulder. A crewman held up two fingers. Two minutes. Mack took a deep breath and put his hand on his pistol. A last resort if captured. He wasn't afraid of death. He died inside a long time ago.

The helicopter hovered over the drop zone kicking up sand. Mack unfastened the seat harness and jumped to the ground. Immediately, the helicopter turned and disappeared into the black sky. Images of past missions circled through Mack's mind. As always, he was on this mission alone. No back up. There was no turning back now.

Mack pulled out the map Rippy provided, illuminating it with his red lens flashlight, paying particular attention to the location of the ground motion sensors. Mack navigated to a position six hundred meters from Osterman's mansion.

Through night vision goggles, he could see floodlights shining on concrete walls beyond the barbed-wire perimeter fence. *This place was more than a mansion. It was a fortress.* As he surveyed the guard towers along the fence, he remembered his commander's last instruction. "Don't get captured. If you do, it means certain death. We can't help you, and Osterman has a nasty way of dealing with enemies."

Mack took out his military knife and dug a shallow hole in the compacted stone road. He rigged the explosives with a cell phone and covered up the charges. Moving to a spot several hundred meters north of the road, he had a clear view of the target.

According to Rippy, Osterman was responsible for numerous assassinations, kidnappings, and torture of anyone who interfered with his illegal drug trade. He was ruthless. If Rippy was right, Osterman would be leaving his ranch in an armored limo at 11 p.m. to settle a turf war involving the sale of narcotics in Los Angeles. The trouble started when Osterman eliminated a top lieutenant in the Russian mob that had been infringing upon his territory.

Mack had already tested the two cell phones, calculating the time that it took from initial call to reception by the second phone. Not knowing the exact speed of Osterman's vehicle, he would have to judge the distance and time with absolute precision. One second too early or too late would mean mission failure. Mack set his watch countdown timer for three seconds. He was ready.

- - -

Becker watched as Osterman picked up a rusty hammer and raised it into the air. He had seen Osterman use this hammer on many victims before.

"Tell me what I want to know," Osterman said.

"I told you. I don't know what you are talking about." The man chained to a steel bed frame tried to wriggle free, but it was futile.

Becker saw the fear in the man's eyes as Osterman put a hand on a bloody and mangled leg.

"You want me to break your other leg too?"

"No. I've told you everything I know. Please let me go."

Osterman twisted the leg violently back and forth. As the man screamed out in pain, a sick smile crossed Osterman's pointy face.

"No one can hear you—you're in the middle of nowhere. You have one last chance. Tell me what I want to know or you'll never leave this mansion alive."

"I am not a Fed."

Osterman looked at Becker and gave him a nod. Becker understood. The man was an undercover federal agent.

"I'll take care of it."

"See that you do. No loose ends," Osterman said as he hobbled out of the room.

- - -

Mack lay motionless on the ground behind a small sand berm. Through the night vision scope, he observed a tall, thin man walk out of the mansion's marbled entrance and limp towards a black limousine. This man matched the description of Osterman in the dossier, right down to the injured leg from a failed assassination by a rival drug lord. Mack watched his target bend over and squeeze himself into the waiting vehicle.

The stone road leaving the ranch was short of two miles long. Three minutes until it reached the detonation spot. Mack quickly assessed the distance and selected a point on the road where the limo would cross and he would make the call.

The limo approached the detonation spot, kicking up dust as it traveled along the gravel road. As it crossed the selection point, Mack dialed the cell phone. A huge explosion and fireball erupted from beneath the road. The bomb had found its target. A second later, the shock wave passed over him making his ears ring. A cold, dead silence filled the air, and then he felt everything going dark.

As he lay on the ground, Mack could see his mother walking to her car as he himself had rushed towards her until she had held up her hand. "*Not today, Johnny.*" As she got in the car and started the engine, she smiled at him just before the explosion. He had made a promise that day his mother was murdered. *I will track them all down. They will pay with their lives.*

Mack regained consciousness. He didn't know how long he had been out. It took a few seconds before he realized what had happened. He had miscalculated the amount of explosive he used.

Mack shook the cobwebs from his mind and looked through the goggles to survey the damage. The only recognizable parts were the engine and a couple of tires.

I'd better get out of here before they come looking for me. Time was running out. The chopper would be back soon. Making his way back to the extraction point, he tried his best to retrace his footsteps.

He wondered if he had been lucky enough to avoid the sensors. The sirens assured him that he had not. Mack ran towards the landing zone, hoping Rippy and the chopper would be waiting. He heard men shouting and the distinctive bark of large guard dogs. He had a head start on them. He could make it if his ride would be waiting. He might be able to avoid the guards, but he couldn't avoid the dogs for long.

Mack ran as fast as he could but his legs betrayed him. He had tried to keep in shape, but age was definitely a factor. Cresting the hill, he hoped to see the helicopter, but all he saw was darkness. He stopped for a second and looked around. Nothing but open land.

Hearing vehicles approaching, he tried to hide himself in a

small crevice. *Where was that damn helicopter?*

"You. Over there. Don't move." A security guard was pointing an M-4 Carbine at Mack's head.

"Damn," Mack said. He stood up with his hands in the air. When he spun around, the guard moved to grab him. Before the guard could react, Mack pulled his Glock from its holster and dropped him with two quick shots. He paused and sprinted towards the sound of rotor blades mashing the air. The helicopter landed on the spot where he jumped out earlier. He ran fast as he could, but his legs felt like two steel beams. Moments before he reached the aircraft, bullets struck its side and the helicopter started to lift off. Lunging with his last ounce of energy, Mack grabbed the skids and pulled himself inside the helicopter as it disappeared into the dark night.

CHAPTER TWO

OSTERMAN'S RANCH
2330 Hours
20 December

"How the hell did this happen?" shouted Becker. "Who was responsible for security tonight?"

No one spoke up. Becker looked around at the armed security guards sitting at computer stations, the monitors showing images inside and outside the mansion.

"Don't jerk me around. Someone screwed up and I'm going to find out who it was. Now, I'm going to ask one last time. Who was responsible for security tonight?"

"I was."

Becker turned around, his green eyes blazing at a small-framed man in a black uniform.

"Oh, so it was you, Mosely? How the hell did someone get through our perimeter? Weren't you at your post?"

"Everything was calm until that big explosion. Only then did we pick up something from the sensors." Mosely hung his head, staring at the ground.

"Where's Johnson?" screamed Becker. "Get me the head of security."

The guards scattered, and in a few minutes Blain Johnson was heading towards him.

"Mr. Becker, I found these at the explosion sight," Johnson said handing some charred pieces of black plastic to Becker.

Becker got a strong whiff of gunpowder as he examined the

items. "What the heck is this?"

"Pieces from some type of remote-control device, possibly a cell phone. Whoever set off the explosion did so at a distance and probably within visual range of the limo. This was no small-time job. We're dealing with real professionals." Johnson pulled out a stack of pictures and handed them to Becker.

"These are the pictures from the night vision cameras. Here is a close-up of the guy who penetrated our perimeter. He's probably the link between the explosion and the helicopter."

Becker stared at the photograph of a burly, middle-aged guy with black hair, cut military close, and chiseled cheekbones. Becker didn't recognize him, which created an even bigger problem.

"Another Fed?" Becker asked.

"Unlikely. Feds don't go around killing people. Probably the Russian mob."

"What about the other fed. He still in the basement?"

"He's still alive. Barely," Johnson said.

Becker pushed past Johnson and yanked open the security room door. "Follow me."

At the bottom of a metal stairwell, Becker walked down a long corridor, dimly lit by three light bulbs that cast ghostly shadows onto the dark-grey walls. A damp smell permeated the concrete hallway.

"Open it."

Johnson pulled out a key and inserted it into a single deadbolt lock on the grey steel door and then stepped aside for Becker to enter.

A single bulb, dangled from the ceiling, above a man strapped to a metal bed frame. Becker pulled out the photograph and shoved it in front of the man's face. "Who is this?"

The man opened his eyes slowly and looked at the photograph.

"Who is this?" Becker placed his hand on the man's injured leg, twisting it farther and farther until the man spoke.

"I never saw him before."

"Look again."

The man stared at the photograph. "I don't know him."

Becker turned and left the room with Johnson closely behind.

"Shoot him full of dope and dump him on the main highway."

"Let him go?"

"You heard me, Johnson. Get him out of here."

"But Osterman…"

"Osterman's dead. I'm in charge now." Becker knew that the Feds would relentlessly pursue anyone who injured one of their agents. They'd be coming for him, but right now he had bigger threats to deal with.

"Find out who this guy is. I want him. Preferably alive, but dead will do," Becker said throwing the pictures at Johnson.

Becker had his own challenges. With Osterman dead, there would be a huge power vacuum. He needed to keep the organization together. As Osterman's second in command, Becker hoped the regional bosses would choose him as the next kingpin.

CHAPTER THREE

Mack was back at the hotel trying to put the incident in some sort of order. He needed to get his act together. Times had changed and so had the technology. What was once only available to the good guys was now available to everyone. He needed a different approach. From now on, all his targets would be treated like a sophisticated enemy. The phone rang. It was Rippy.

"Good job, Mack. Understand you had a little problem though. Glad to see everything turned out all right. Your next assignment is in the pre-arranged location, along with instructions for obtaining support and equipment. Good luck. I'll talk to you after mission completion."

The phone went dead. It was better that way.

Mack removed the top drawer of the cherry hotel dresser. Turning the drawer over, he saw a brown envelope taped to the bottom. Obviously, Rippy had it placed there while he was on the mission. In large black lettering, the envelope read *"Project Number Two."* Mack opened the envelope and emptied the contents. Just as the previous mission, there were photographs of the intended target. This time however, there were two large stacks of hundred dollar bills. This was the first time that he had used his assassination skills for money. Mack wondered whether he had made the right decision.

Only a week had gone by since his first meeting with Colonel Rippy. Mack was initially suspicious when Rippy proffered the idea of eliminating twelve targets for money, but these suspicions subsided when Rippy mentioned *Operation Jungle Fever*, a highly classified government covert operation that used assassinations to eliminate enemies of the United States. Only those with the highest security clearance and the need to know would even be aware that operation had ever existed.

When Mack accepted the current assignment to revitalize the operation, Rippy told him the mission would cease when twelve targets were eliminated. Mack knew that Rippy played on his sense of great loyalty, but Mack could not refuse the government's request for service despite the current political situation. Mack was a government assassin, not a politician. Unless something changed, he would follow orders and complete the mission.

Mack looked at the photographs. They depicted an older, distinguished-looking gentleman with gray hair and bifocals. He flipped the photo over and read the information on the back:

Richard Muhler, age 61
Chief Executive Officer, Muhler Chemical Corporation
5423 East Muhler Avenue, Bellevue WA
Selected for termination

This time, there was no listing of the crimes committed by the target. He would spend a couple of days surveying Muhler and then strike. If he wanted to survive the next mission, he needed to plan for every detail this time.

SEATTLE, WASHINGTON
1400 Hours
23 December

Mack was met at the Seattle airport by one of "Rippy's Raiders", the name he had given to Rippy's support guys. After loading the equipment into a dark gray pickup truck, he drove south on Interstate 5 towards Olympia.

Mack followed Rippy's directions to an old motel, where used syringes and condom wrappers littered its parking lot. As disgusted as he was, he knew it was the perfect place to avoid unwanted attention. The room was damp and musty. Mack took one look at the saggy bed and stain-covered comforter. He decided to sleep in the faux-leather chair. With luck, he wouldn't be staying in this dump for long.

Mack sat in the dark, troubled by the recent vision of his mother. He was no closer now to finding her killers than he was when he started his quest thirty years earlier. Revenge once again began to consume him. He tugged at his mother's pink crystal amulet hanging around his neck. He found it in the rubble of the explosion. His thoughts turned to his mother. Since her death, Mack had been consumed with finding her murderers.

Early the next morning, Mack jumped in his pickup and drove out to Muhler Chemical Corporation in Tacoma. Mack was impressed by the large, mirrored-glass structure. According to the dossier, Muhler would be driving either a black sedan or a silver convertible. Scanning the parking lot, Mack located a black sedan near the front entrance. The license plate number matched the information in the dossier. *Not a good place for the attack.* It was too well lit, and the company had several roving security guards.

He would wait for Muhler, then follow him to find a better place to eliminate him.

Mack pulled into an empty spot on the far side of the lot. He sat in the truck keeping a constant vigil on the movements of people entering and leaving the building. Out of the corner of his eye, he caught an image of a male figure approaching his vehicle.

"What's going on here?" A middle-aged man dressed in a grey uniform, his stomach hanging over a large black belt, stood next to the truck.

"What's the problem, officer?"

"Don't know yet? You've been parked here for quite some time. You an employee? I don't see a parking pass."

"Nah…not yet."

Mack noticed the puzzled look on the security guard's face.

"I'm looking for work. Heard this place is hiring."

"Don't know where you heard that. Our HR department is in Olympia. Suggest you move along." The guard tapped his old revolver holstered around his fat waist.

"That sounds like good advice." Mack started the truck and drove towards the parking lot exit. As he passed the front of the building, he saw a man fitting the description of Muhler emerge from the building and walk to the black sedan. He was a lot bigger than Mack imagined. Mack pulled out the photograph of Muhler and compared it to the man walking towards the vehicle. It was Muhler all right.

Muhler drove out of the parking lot with Mack closely behind. Following Muhler through the streets of Tacoma, they arrived in front of a large Victorian-style home. Muhler went into the home and returned shortly with a teenage boy by his side. The boy looked like any other brown-haired, blue-eyed teenager, Mack thought, but something was not quite right. The lack of expression in the boy's face. The way he walked.

Must be the guy's kid. But this guy was too old to have a kid that age. Mack followed Muhler and the young boy to a residence in Bellevue. As the car turned into a driveway, Mack pulled to the side of the road, just close enough to get a good look at the layout. Black scroll lettering on the grey stone mailbox: *333 Forest Lane.* This was Muhler's home.

Muhler guided the young man towards the entrance of the massive stone home, his hand on the buttocks of the young boy. Mack's face flamed with anger. There was nothing lower in this world than a guy like that. Mack needed to see what was going on inside. It would make a difference in the way he was going to kill him.

Making his way across the street, Mack walked past the entrance gates. He crouched down beside the Lexus, noticing that one of the side windows provided a narrow view of Muhler's living room. The boy was sitting on a red Persian carpet near the large brick fireplace with Muhler screaming at him.

"You didn't do what I told you to. You've been very bad and you need to be punished."

Muhler picked up a whip off the coffee table and raised it to strike the boy.

"Please don't hurt me. I'll do whatever you want." The boy's voice cracked and tears began to fill his eyes.

Mack's entire body clenched tightly. This was more than he could stand. Picking up a large rock, he tossed it through the window. He wanted to snuff the life out of Muhler now, but not with the boy there. As the window shattered, Mack sprinted back to his truck. Muhler opened the front door and went outside to survey the damage. Holding the rock with both hands, he stared at the broken window.

"Damn punk kids," Muhler said. "Let me get my hands on you. You'll pay for this."

Muhler re-entered the house and returned a short time later with the boy, pushing him ahead.

"Move. Keep going. Get in the car."

"Stop kicking me. I'm going. I'm going."

"Shut up and get in the car." Muhler pushed the boy again, this time hard enough to knock him down.

"Get up."

When the boy didn't get up quickly enough, Muhler grabbed him by the arm and yanked him to his feet. The kid let out a heart-breaking scream.

It took every bit of self-control Mack could muster. *Your day is coming Muhler.*

Muhler opened the door and pushed the young boy into the passenger side. He then walked around the back of the car, not seeming to care if anyone was watching. As he drove away, Mack followed at a safe distance. After Muhler dropped the boy off, Mack didn't bother following him. He knew where he was going to strike. He just needed to figure out the method of termination.

Once the boy went into the house, Mack walked up and rang the bell. A thin white man dressed in spandex pants and sporting bleach blonde hair, answered the door.

"May I help you?"

Mack almost puked. "Yeah, I'm looking for a companion."

"What do you mean?"

"Look, they said that I can find young boys here. If you don't want my business, I'll go somewhere else."

"You a cop? You look like a cop."

"If I was a cop, you'd be under arrest right now," Mack shot back.

"Well, you don't have to get so huffy."

Mack wanted to choke the life out of this guy, but he needed him.

"My name is Jimmy. I can show you around. Tell me if you see anything you like."

Mack smiled back. He was going to enjoy cleaning this place up. Walking through the house, he noticed about ten young boys, all average-looking except that not one of them smiled. Their expressionless faces and trance-like state were the same of the boy Muhler had taken to his home. *These boys were being sedated. And I have a good idea who was doing it.* He started to formulate a plan.

"I would like a red-haired one," Mack said.

"I only have one boy with red hair. You can't take him now. We are closed for the day. If you want, you can come get him tomorrow, but you'll have to pay in advance."

"Fine, I'll come for him tomorrow morning."

"Suit yourself, honey. I'll be here."

Mack left the house and drove back to the hotel. He didn't risk going to Muhler's now in case the police were called to investigate the broken window. He would wait until tomorrow to strike.

This time, Mack slept better. The horrible images, buried for all those years and re-ignited by Rippy's call, started to subside. Mack thought there were times he would have benefited from the help of a shrink, but because of the high secrecy of the military operations, he couldn't tell anyone about it. Emotions inside of him kept silent for more than thirty years. He knew this was the reason that he never married and had no friends. Being back in "operational status" was the best medicine for him.

Mack woke early the next morning and opened the motel-room shades to a sky the color of fireplace ashes anchored with low-hanging clouds that looked like bands of dirty cotton balls. The night's rain had slowed to an annoying mist. Mack got dressed, put on a lightweight stocking cap and a green and black jacket. He picked up, racked the slide on a .22 caliber pistol, and then slid it into his jacket pocket.

After dressing, Mack found a place to have breakfast. He had been to the Seattle area in the late 1990s, and could not believe how much the area had changed. He had often thought about moving there, but each time dismissed the idea. After he terminated Muhler, and maybe his little "pal," Jimmy, he knew he couldn't return. Mack ordered two eggs, bacon, toast, and coffee for breakfast. Purchasing a newspaper from the rack in the restaurant foyer, he scanned the police log. In a small entry, Mack found what he was looking for. The police log indicated that vandals smashed a window in a home belonging to Richard Muhler, 333 Forest Lane, Bellevue WA. Mack laughed. *I've been called many a name, but never a "vandal".*

After breakfast, Mack headed to the Victorian house. As he drove past, he remembered the look of despair and hopelessness in the young boys' eyes.

There was only one entrance facing the street and another entrance at the rear of the residence near a short gravel driveway. Large pine trees in the back of the house cast eerie shadows as the sun struggled to shine through the ash-colored clouds. Because the rear entrance provided greater concealment, he would enter the house from the front and exit through the rear, lessening the chances of being seen. He parked his truck a block away from the rear of the residence and walked up to the house and rang the bell. Jimmy was dressed in the same spandex pants, but this time he had a scarf tied around his waist as a belt.

"Come on in, Mister . . .? Uh, I didn't get your name."

"That's because I didn't give it to you," Mack snapped back.

Mack quickly assessed the situation. Other than the young boys, he was alone with this poor excuse for a human. "Where's the boy you promised me?"

When Jimmy turned to walk away, Mack pulled his pistol and struck him on the side of his head, dropping Jimmy to his knees.

"You tell me who your boss is, and I won't kill you."

"Let me go. Let me go."

Mack ripped the scarf from Jimmy's waist and twisted it around his neck.

"You better tell me what I want to know," Mack said, twisting the scarf tighter with each word.

As Jimmy started to lose consciousness, Mack released the tension on the scarf.

"OK, OK, I'll talk. Just don't kill me."

"First the answer. Who runs this place?"

"I don't know," said Jimmy between fits of coughing.

Mack started tightening the scarf around Jimmy's neck again, only loose enough so he could still talk.

"You telling me the truth, or just telling me crap to save your scrawny neck?"

"Muhler. He's the guy who set this up. I just get paid to run it."

He wanted to kill this pig, but if Jimmy went to prison, he would get what was coming to him. Inmates don't like child molesters.

"Where is the dope that you've been giving these boys?" Mack shouted. "Where is it?"

Mack yanked Jimmy to his feet and twisted his arm back so far that the man let out a loud scream.

"Stop it, you're hurting me." Jimmy squealed.

"Shut up." Mack twisted his arm farther. "Show me where the dope is. Now."

"It's in the kitchen." Jimmy's voice dropped to a whisper.

Down a hall past closed doors, Mack clamped Jimmy's arm as the jerk led him to the back of the house. The only sound was their footsteps and Jimmy's occasional whimper.

The kitchen cabinets, once white, were now a putrid yellow from the years of cigarette smoke. Mack's feet stuck to the floor with each step as he escorted Jimmy to the cabinets.

"Which cabinet?" Mack said sternly, his voice growing more impatient with each passing moment.

Jimmy pointed to the cabinet on top of the refrigerator.

"Do it," Mack said. "Now. And no funny stuff."

Jimmy opened the cabinet and removed several large white bottles of prescription medicine.

"Here. Here they are, now let me go."

Mack grabbed the bottles and struck Jimmy again with his pistol, knocking him unconscious. *Maybe it was time for this piece of garbage to get a taste of his own medicine.* Mack finished taking care of Jimmy and called the police. He had barely hung up the phone when he heard sirens. He slipped out the rear entrance and took cover along the large pine trees. He walked the block to his truck and drove away. In the rear-view mirror, Mack watched two police cars pull up to the house.

Back in his motel room, he turned on the television. A local channel caught his attention. Mack turned up the volume. An attractive brunette reporter was live on the scene.

"Chief, can you tell us what happened here today?"

"Yes, as the facts are coming in, it appears as though we located a potential sex-slave operation using young boys ranging in age from 10 to 13. Well, their age is pretty much a guess until we determine their identities. From what we can initially gather, these young boys were being offered for the pleasure of adult men."

"What makes you believe that these boys were being used as sex slaves for adult men?" asked the newscaster.

"This is our initial opinion. Preliminary medical examinations of two of the young boys reveal evidence of sexual assault. We will know more once we interview the young boys that we located inside the house. We have not been able to interview any of the boys yet because they appear to be under the influence of some kind of narcotic. We found a large, half-empty bottle of them in the kitchen of the residence."

"Was there anyone else in the house? Anyone caring for the boys?"

"We found one adult male inside the residence. He was unconscious and had marks on his necks which could have been caused by a scarf located nearby, which we believe is his."

"Have you questioned him?"

"We have not yet been able to question the adult male. He has been taken to the local hospital for a possible drug overdose."

"What makes you suspect a drug overdose?"

"Paramedics found nearly 40 capsules inside of the man's stomach."

"Any idea why he would do that?"

"At this point, all I can do is speculate. We suspect he tried to strangle himself, and when that didn't work, he took the pills. We also found partially crushed capsules in his hand. Unless I miss my guess, the adult man was involved in this child-slave operation."

"I understand that you got a call informing you of this situation?"

"That's correct. We received a call that there were young boys being held against their will at this residence."

"Do you know who made that call? Is this person also involved?"

"No, we don't know who made the call. To be honest with you, the only reason that I would like to know who made the call is to shake his hand. He saved these boys."

Mack's cell phone started to ring. He snapped off the television and recognized the incoming number.

"What kind of stunt was that?"

"What are you talking about?" Mack replied.

"You know darn well what I'm talking about. It's all over the news. Your assignment is Muhler. Once the police question that guy, they will know Muhler was involved. If they get to him before you do, the mission will be a failure. See that they don't."

"Understood," Mack said as he hung up the phone.

CHAPTER FOUR

OSTERMAN'S RANCH
0900 Hours
23 December

Becker sat in Osterman's office at a large, mahogany desk. He recalled the numerous times he had stood in front of this desk with Osterman giving him orders on how to carry out the drug trafficking activities. Now with Osterman gone, Becker was sitting behind the desk giving out the same type of orders. The regional bosses once had respect for Osterman, but Becker had yet to earn their respect. He knew if he wasn't careful, he could find himself dead by the hands of one of these bosses. He also worried about who eliminated Osterman. He was small potatoes, but if he managed to take over as the new boss, he could be setting himself up for the same scenario as Osterman. He needed to think things through. First he would find out who killed Osterman, then deal with the regional bosses. *If I can catch the guys that got Osterman, I could gain their respect.* Becker's thoughts were interrupted when he heard a knock at the door.

"Who is it?"

"Sir, it's Johnson."

"Enter."

Johnson opened the door and made his way to where Becker was seated.

"Johnson, tell me you know who was behind the hit."

"Sir, we've run the picture with our people back east. So far, we haven't been able to come up with anything. We've got a contact inside the CIA and he's got his ear to the wall for any tidbit of information. I'm confident that we'll know who this guy is in four or five days."

"You've got two days, Johnson. You'd better find out who this guy is. No excuses."

Johnson left Becker and walked to his office. He closed the door and telephoned his connection at the CIA.

"Wilson, this is Johnson. Any word on my request?"

"Nah, not yet. We ran the picture you sent me through our databases and there's a problem."

"Yeah? What kind of problem?"

"The guy in the picture you sent me doesn't exist. He's deceased."

"What are you talking about? He's not dead, we have him on camera."

"Maybe the same guy, but I doubt it. I double checked the photo with a friend at the Pentagon. Whoever he is, I don't want him after me."

"Will you just tell me who this man is? I'll deal with him. We can handle one person."

"That's what I've been trying to tell you. My friend at the Pentagon is in big trouble. When he ran the photo, the computer denied him access and alarmed security. I can't help you anymore."

"Hey, you owe me Wilson. Don't forget the hand that feeds you. The boss won't be happy to hear this. I'm glad I'm not in your shoes."

"If this guy is after you, I'm glad I'm not in your shoes."

Johnson didn't know what to say. Becker was not going to like the news. He was merciless when it came to failures.

OUTSIDE THE HOME OF RICHARD MUHLER
333 FOREST LANE, BELLEVUE WA
CHRISTMAS DAY
0500 HOURS

John Mack stood across the street from the home. Through the black metal gates, he could see the front of the home, adorned with Christmas decorations. In the two-story glass window in the center of the house, stood a large pine tree decorated with soft glowing lights and rings of garland and tinsel. Atop the tree, sat an angel adorned in a white gown, holding two glowing, lighted candles. *Peace on Earth, Goodwill towards Men. What a bunch of crap. This guy doesn't deserve goodwill or peace. The world needs to know how evil this guy is and I know just the way to do it.*

The gates were designed to prevent vehicles from entering. Tall brick walls on both sides made scaling them difficult, if not impossible. Luscious green hedgerows provided a narrow opening to enter the premises. Moving through the bushes, Mack approached the home from the side. Carefully moving within the shadows, he made it to the garage without setting off any of the floodlight sensors.

During military training, Mack had learned to never assume. He had been given thirty seconds to manipulate a locked door and succeeded in just under the time limit. He was proud of his accomplishment until he learned that the door had never been locked. Mack pulled a pick from his jacket in case he needed to manipulate the lock leading into Muhler's garage. He grabbed the door knob and gave it a quick turn. Success. His training had paid off again.

Mack slipped the pick in his pocket and pushed the door open a few inches, waiting for any alarms. He knew that the main security panel would be located near the entry way into the home. Mack pushed the door open a bit more and entered the garage, keeping within the shadows. He scanned the garage looking for a motion sensor. Finding none, Mack was confident that it was safe to move. Muhler's black sedan was parked alongside a silver convertible.

Mack quickly made his way across the garage, moving with both speed and purpose. The entry to the main portion of the house was a steel door equipped with a deadlock bolt. Three wooden steps led from the garage floor to the threshold of the door. Mack carefully stepped on the first step, with ever increasing body weight, listening for any squeaks. Hearing none, he did the same on the second and third step. Now just inches away from the entry door, he grabbed the knob and twisted ever so slightly. The door knob turned. *Still two obstacles; the deadbolt and the alarm.*

Mack pushed on the door. It opened slightly. *Past the deadbolt. Now, if I can move slowly enough, I can get inside without setting off the alarm.* With the door open a third of the way, Mack dropped to his belly and pulled himself into the house. Rolling onto his back he scanned the walls for the security system.

On the wall he spotted the panel. Mack scanned the rest of the area looking for any motion detectors, finding one in a corner of the room.

Still on his on his back, Mack quickly raised his arm straight up breaking the sensor threshold. The green LED light quickly changed to red indicating movement. *No alarms. So far, so good.* Mack quickly jumped to his feet and quietly closed the door behind him.

Rippy's information indicated Muhler lived alone. A short

corridor led to a massive kitchen area. Mack looked quickly around for pet food bowls. As good as Mack was, even a small dog would betray his presence and alarm Muhler.

Mack moved through the kitchen and into the great room. A large Christmas tree stood majestically in the center, its thousands of colored lights twinkling on an off. A heavy, but pleasant smell of evergreen permeated the room.

Opposite the large tree rose a grand staircase. Mack climbed the stairs, quickly reaching the top. A hallway to the right and one to the left. *Which way to go?* Mack stood still for a second and listened. *What's that noise?* Snoring was coming from his left, through a partially opened doorway. Making his way down the hallway, he watched carefully at each door he passed.

Mack entered the room, remaining motionless, letting his eyes adjust to the darkness. Ever since Mack was a child, he had excellent night vision. His enlarged pupils allowed more light than typical to enter his eyes, enabling him to see much better in the dark than most people.

Muhler was face down on a king sized canopy bed. Mack approached and pulled out the .22 caliber handgun. Grabbing one of the pillows, Mack removed the pillow case. With Muhler still snoring loudly, he put the pistol against Muhler's head, but instead of pulling the trigger, he pushed the gun hard against the temple region. Muhler winced and tried to get up, but his head was pinned against the bed.

"What the...?"

"Shut up." Mack quickly grabbed the pillow case and pulled it over Muhler's head, pulling it tight around Muhler' neck.

"What's going on? Who are you? What do you want? Let me go."

"If you say one more word, I swear to God I will shoot you right here, right now."

Muhler's breathing became rapid and shallow. Mack yanked on the pillow case, pulling Muhler upright.

"Let's go," Mack said.

Muhler was mumbling something under his breath, but Mack didn't care what he had to say. Mack slipped the pistol back into his pocket, grabbed Muhler's right arm and twisted it behind his back. Using his left arm to hold the pillow case around Muhler's neck and his right arm to keep the arm pinned behind his back, Mack guided him out of the bedroom and to the stairway.

"Stairs," Mack said loudly.

Muhler was in mid-stride, his right foot close to the first step. He started to lose his balance, but Mack yanked him back. Muhler's knees started to buckle, but Mack just twisted his arm harder, straightening him back up. As they walked through the great room, Muhler struggled, attempting to free himself of Mack's grip. Mack shoved him to the ground.

"That's for the little boy you were kicking the other day." Kicking Muhler harder with each word.

"Stop. You're hurting me."

"And this is for all the boys you hurt," Mack said as he yanked Muhler back to his feet and led him out to the garage.

Mack opened the driver side door of the sedan and pushed Muhler inside. Mack put Muhler in a choke hold and held it until he became unconscious. Locating a vacuum cleaner on the far side of the garage, he grabbed the hose and inserted one end into the exhaust pipe and the other end into the partially opened driver's window.

While the deadly exhaust gases from the tailpipe flowed into the driver's compartment, Mack pulled a photograph of Muhler and the young naked boy that Mack had taken just prior to throwing the rock through the window. He placed the photograph on the dash of the vehicle, and waited long enough for the lethal fumes to completely fill the inside.

"Sweet dreams," Mack said as he left the garage.

Back in his hotel room, he tried to piece together what connection, if any, Osterman had with Muhler. Osterman was a major drug dealer, and Muhler was a sexual predator. Both men were wealthy, in their early sixties, and Caucasian. Mack could understand why the government would want to eliminate Osterman; they had tried every legal method to take him down and failed.

But why did they use me to take down Muhler? They could've done surveillance and discovered the same thing I did. Doesn't make sense. Mack's thoughts were interrupted when he saw Muhler's home flash across the television. *"Breaking News: Chemical Company CEO takes his own life...suspected of running the Tacoma child sex-slave operation discovered last week."* Mack turned up the volume.

CHAPTER FIVE

OSTERMAN'S RANCH
1430 hours
26 DECEMBER

In a few short hours, regional bosses of the drug cartel would be arriving at the ranch, and they wanted answers as to who killed Osterman—answers Becker did not have. His contacts at the CIA and the Pentagon had gone underground. The government was probably already investigating the unauthorized access to information by Wilson's friend. Becker was glad he had safeguards in place to make it difficult, if not impossible, for the feds to trace the information request back to him. He used prepaid cell phones registered in fictitious names with fake addresses and destroyed them after the placing the calls to the CIA and Pentagon. Their SIMM cards would never be traced or found.

When the phone on Osterman's desk rang, Becker was pacing back and forth, trying to come up with what he was going to tell the bosses.

"Hello?"

"Mr. Becker? This is James Black. I have information on the dirt sample you sent us."

"Go ahead, I'm listening."

"Each explosive leaves a chemical fingerprint of its origin. My analysis has concluded that the explosive used in the blast was PVV-5A plastic explosive."

"That's supposed to mean something?"

"It is has particular significance because this material is

widely used by Russia and its military allies."

"Can anyone get their hands on this stuff?" asked Becker.

"Extremely uncommon here in the U.S. It is much easier to get your hands on C-4. C-4 is the most common explosive."

A few months back, Osterman had met with leaders of a Russian-based organized crime syndicate. Osterman left the meeting after they threatened to kill him if he didn't cut them in on a piece of the action.

Becker was a life-long criminal. Before he was 18 years old, he had committed numerous aggravated assaults, robberies, burglaries, thefts and drug related offenses. Most he committed just for the excitement.

It was arson that sent him to federal prison for several years. Becker had attempted to rob a bank, but didn't make it more than a few feet outside of the bank when the dye packs exploded on the money, making it virtually useless. It was at this point that Becker's violent streak kicked into action. He pulled out a gasoline can from the trunk of his getaway car and went back into the bank.

The tellers, who were traumatized by the initial robbery, panicked when they witnessed Becker pouring gasoline at the entrance to the bank. Becker lit the gasoline on his way out of the bank. The gasoline immediately flared up, nearly burning Becker as he made his way out of the bank. Becker got into his getaway car and started to drive away. Had he left after the dye pack explosion, he most likely would have evaded the police. However, since he took the time to exact revenge on the tellers, he didn't get far before being apprehended. Luckily for those inside of the bank, the automatic sprinklers kicked in immediately after the start of the blaze.

Becker's attorney, an experienced public defender, got the

charges reduced from attempted homicide to arson. Becker was sent to federal prison and because of his violent criminal activities, was housed with the most violent offenders. It was during this period of incarceration that Becker made contact with Osterman, who was awaiting trial for drug trafficking. The two quickly became friends and after Becker's release, he went to work for Osterman and the drug cartel.

The regional boss arrived on schedule. Several large, black SUVs pulled into the ranch and parked in front of the house. Guards were stationed in front of the vehicle, and others posted around the perimeter. Becker recognized the man, dressed in a grey designer suit, as Giovanni Calderone, the senior regional boss. His immense girth caused him to waddle like a drunken penguin.

"This way, Mr. Calderone," Becker said, motioning towards the entrance to the mansion.

"Let's get this meeting started."

Becker escorted Calderone to the entertainment room. This meeting, however, was not about entertainment, but fact gathering. A long table, with a chair at each end, had been placed near the center of the room. Becker worried that his fate would be decided at this meeting, more specifically at this table. If he didn't have the answers the boss was looking for, he would be seen as incompetent and might pay the price for it with his life.

"Sit. Now what the hell happened?"

"Well, Osterman was killed by a roadside bomb," Becker said.

"No kidding. We figured that much out for ourselves. Where's the son-of-a-bitch that killed him?"

"Unfortunately, we haven't been able to catch him yet," Becker said looking the boss directly in the eye. Becker knew that if he appeared weak, he was a dead man. There was a fine line between being arrogant and being respectful. He figured that the best approach was to keep his answers short and to the point. He would not speculate unless Calderone asked him to.

"Unfortunate for you," the boss replied. "You at least know who this guy is, right?"

"We have people working on it," Becker said not making eye-contact.

"Working on it? Working on it? I don't want to hear that. You had better find this guy, and find this guy quick. I want him, and anyone else involved, dealt with now."

"There is a lot that we don't know at this point, but I can tell you what we found out so far," Becker said calmly.

"OK. Frickin' amuse me."

"The laboratory determined that the explosive material used in the blast was PVV-5A plastic explosive—"

"So frickin' what?"

"What I was about to tell you …" Becker shot a displeased glance but caught himself and regained his composure. "That particular plastic explosive is manufactured by the Soviet Union. It is extremely difficult to obtain in the United States."

"Frickin' commie bastards."

"It appears that way," Becker said. "The Russian mob had threatened to kill Osterman recently. They don't make idle threats."

"I'm going to kill each one of them schmucks … we don't make idle threats either."

"Well, there is another possibility."

Calderone leaned in, his eyes focusing on Becker.

"It could be the U.S. government."

"You lost your frickin' marbles. The frickin' U.S.

Government? I heard of some paranoid conspiracy crap before, but this is frickin' ludicrous."

"The U.S. has the ability to obtain the PVV-5A plastic explosive and the picture that we have drew major attention at the CIA and the Pentagon."

"You gotta a frickin' picture of this guy? You tell me all this crap about Russians and government conspiracies, and now you tell us that you have a picture of this schmuck?"

Becker placed a large photograph, taken by the surveillance cameras soon after the explosion, in front of Calderone. The image was enlarged several times, each time slightly distorting the image.

"Looks like a frickin' Russian to me."

"We lost our contact at the CIA and Pentagon. However, we have another option which may provide some results."

"Well, you think I'm a frickin' mind reader?"

Becker was getting seriously annoyed. "We have a contact at the Department of Transportation. Whenever someone transfers an out-of-state license, the photo is run through the driver's license database using facial recognition software to ensure nobody can get licenses under multiple names. We sent the picture to our contact just prior to your arrival. We are waiting to see if we get a hit on the photo."

"You better hope that they come up with something," the boss spouted.

"I'll let you know as soon as we hear. Now, how about drinks and entertainment?"

Smiling, Becker nodded to one of his underlings, and a parade of female dancers entered the room. Heather was in Calderone's lap, fondling his fleshy earlobe and flashing her cleavage in his face. Next minute, she was leading him down the hall. Becker could count on Heather to keep Calderone busy while he obtained the results of the license photo comparison. With luck, the boss would be entertained until morning.

Becker finished his scotch whiskey and motioned for one of the three remaining women. A dark-haired woman of Spanish descent walked over to Becker's chair. He whispered into her ear and the woman smiled, then nodded acknowledgement. Becker followed her to a vacant bedroom. As he took off his clothes and was ready to jump into bed, a knock came at the door.

"Who the hell is it?"

"We got the information that you were waiting for from the Department of Transportation."

"Your friggin' timing is perfect. Hang on . . . I'll be right there," Becker said as he started putting on his clothes.

"Sorry sir," the voice said. "They said to tell you as soon as we knew."

Becker finished putting on his clothes and opened the door. A security guard held out several sheets of computer printouts. Becker grabbed the papers and growled. The guard didn't flinch, only looked down at the floor, turned and walked away. He poked his head into the bedroom.

"I've got business to take care of. I'll be back in a while; don't start without me." Becker winked at the woman.

Becker marched his way to the compound's security office located on the main floor of the mansion. Becker placed his right thumb on the scanner. The cipher lock's LCD display illuminated a touch screen keypad. Becker entered in his seven-digit PIN, and the door lock clicked open.

The security room was the size of a small restaraunt. On the long wall facing the doorway were twelve video monitors depicting the images from the numerous surveillance cameras both inside the mansion and throughout the grounds. Seated in front of these monitors were two armed, uniformed security guards. Both guards were watching the monitors that depicted Calderone with his female companion, alternately panning and zooming the camera lens.

"I hope you're recording that." Becker pointed to the video monitors.

"Yes, sir. Both audio and video."

"Don't let me catch you watching me."

"No, sir, the camera to that bedroom was turned off as soon as you entered the room."

Becker kept the recordings of his guest's sexual encounters to use as blackmail. Numerous influential and politically connected men were "entertained" at Osterman's ranch. On more than one occasion, short video clips of these men's encounters had been emailed to influence or persuade them to comply with Osterman's requests. Now that Osterman was dead, Becker had full access and control over these blackmail videos.

"Tell Johnson I want to see him," Becker bellowed.

"Yes, sir." The guard started displaying different camera views in an effort to find Johnson.

Within a few moments, the guard spotted Johnson in the kitchen, stuffing his face with a large piece of chocolate cake. The guard dialed the kitchen's extension.

"Tell Johnson to come to security. Now!" the guard told the chef.

The guard listened to the chef give Johnson the message. Johnson said he would head over as soon as he finished his cake. The guard called the kitchen again.

"Tell Johnson that Becker wants him, and he is ticked off."

Johnson shot out of his chair as if it had been set on fire. Both the guards roared with laughter.

"What's so friggin' funny?" Becker asked.

"Nothing, sir. Johnson should be here any minute."

No sooner than the guard finished the sentence, the sound of Johnson's pounding footsteps could be heard rapidly approaching the security office. Becker opened the door just as Johnson arrived.

"What the heck took you so long?" Becker asked with a slight grin.

Becker knew what the guards had pulled and thought it was rather amusing.

"I got here as quickly as I could," Johnson said, half out of breath. "Did you get the information from the Department of Transportation?"

"Yeah, that's why I'm here. Says here that a facial recognition match was identified for an individual by the name of John Mack, address in Harrisburg, Pennsylvania."

Becker flipped through the pages of the document handed to him earlier and pulled out the driver's license photo of Mack. Becker compared the driver's photo with the images taken by the surveillance cameras on the night that Osterman was killed. Although the surveillance images were green in color from the night vision equipment, the profile image of Mack wearing a black knit cap was strikingly similar to the driver's license photo.

"Good work Johnson," Becker said. "This guy either set the bomb or was somehow involved. Makes no difference one way or another. I want to know who is behind that attack. He's working for someone, someone with connections sufficient to obtain freaking Russian plastic explosives. I want this guy taken alive.

We need him to find out who he is working for. Let's get some men up to this guy's address to conduct some surveillance. We'll have one chance to get him. For now, the element of surprise is on our side."

"We have some connections in New York. We'll have them go to Harrisburg and see what they can find out. I'll call right away and get them headed in that direction."

"Good job, Johnson. There is a girl in number four waiting for me. After you make that call, she's all yours," Becker said with a grin.

Johnson acted like he could not believe his ears. He started walking towards the bedroom, but then transitioned into a full run.

"Record that," Becker said pointing to the image of Johnson inside the bedroom.

CHAPTER SIX

VIRGINIA BEACH, VIRGINIA
1300 Hours
15 May

Mack, receiving his next assignment, proceeded to Virginia. Once again, the target listing would be taped to the bottom of a dresser drawer in his hotel room. Approaching Virginia Beach, he detected the smell of salt air. It took him back to the time when he was training to be a scuba diver.

Mack didn't learn to swim the way most young children did. During a birthday party, some boys learned that he could not swim and threw him into the swimming pool. He almost drowned. Initially he panicked, flailing around and taking water in through his mouth and nose. The more he flailed, the quicker his oxygen supply was being depleted. Moments before he would have blacked out, Mack completely relaxed his body, floated to the surface, and pulled his head up for a few gulps of air. Making his way to the side of the pool, he pulled himself out of the water and left that day with a valuable lesson that had served him well since then. When faced with a life or death situation, panicking makes the situation worse. If you're not so lucky, panicking can get you killed.

Mack's attention snapped back to the present like a bear trap when the car in front of him suddenly braked. His quick reaction kept the SUV from striking the rear of a blue convertible. The license plate read "DIAMONDS." The top was down, easy for Mack to see the two occupants; a dark-tanned man with graying hair with a few remaining strands of jet black and a blonde female. When the woman turned her head to speak to the driver, she gave Mack a frontal view of her striking features. Perfect smile, beautiful blue eyes that seemed to invite you into them. Striking, but graceful too, like a dancer he'd seen on stage once.

Mack pulled alongside the car to get a better look. The man, in his late fifties, wore dark sunglasses and gold rings of all shapes and sizes. On his left hand Mack noticed a unique, golden ring with the symbol of a cross that was encrusted with diamonds in the center and surrounded by black onyx. The man's most obtrusive feature was his nose, which was thick, protruding, and disproportionately large for his face. He glanced briefly as Mack slowly started to pass the convertible.

Sitting higher in the SUV, Mack had a clear view into the passenger compartment of the convertible. Mack turned his attention to the remarkable beautiful blonde in the front passenger seat. At this distance, she was even more attractive than Mack had first realized. She was wearing a tight, white cotton shirt which flattered her curvy features. Her black mini-skirt rode higher than normal in the seated position. At the end of her long, tanned, athletic legs, were a pair of black high heels with sequin accents.

Mack slowed briefly to take in as much of this view as possible, and when he did, the blonde turned and looked Mack in the eye. He gave her a broad smile. Smiling was something that Mack rarely did. The woman returned his smile and turned her head slightly to the left and down, flirting. Mack gave her a wink and smiled even larger. The woman's face turned red. The driver placed his right hand on the woman's bare leg, turned to Mack, and gave him a cocky smirk. He then accelerated, leaving Mack in his dust.

Mack checked into the hotel under the name of Paul Brittan and headed toward the elevator. The hotel was typical, with a lobby pleasantly decorated with ocean-type decorum, and walls painted the color of the blue-green waters. It was the start of the tourist season, with unseasonable warm temperatures in the mid-80s, so Mack blended in perfectly in his shorts, sandals, and T-Shirt.

As Mack entered his room on the twelfth floor, he half expected someone to be inside. He was alone. The room had a great view of the ocean. He stepped onto the patio and the warm, bright sunshine felt good against his body. The beach was packed with tourists swimming, walking, and sunning. Children's laughter carried up to the patio. Parents were helping toddlers build sandcastles, throwing Frisbees to teens, calling after kids to stay out of the deep, warning them of riptides.

Mack knew that this next target would need to be eliminated in a place, and in a manner, where no children would be affected. *I will never have a child experience the trauma that I did.*

He decided to study the target for a day before committing to a specific course of action. Mack then removed the information package from the bottom of the dresser drawer. The typed page with *"Howard Rutherford"* in big, bold letters across the top read *"Selected for termination for the crimes against the United States for violation of Human Rights, slave labor, and ethnic cleansing."* Mack pulled out the photo of the target, sat back, and stared. He had seen this guy before. *This was the guy that he passed in the convertible. The guy with that gorgeous girl.* There was no mistaking that nose.

Mack continued to read the dossier. Rutherford was the president and chief operating officer of the world's largest diamond importer, Rutherford Diamonds. The license plate on the car made sense now. Rutherford has been importing large amounts of diamonds into the United States over the past fifteen years. The diamonds were mined in South Africa where most of the labor came from men, women, and children who were forced to work in the mines or face certain death. Women and children were sexually assaulted and raped on a routine basis.

Mack wondered why these were crimes against the United States. After all, these were not U.S. citizens who were involved. Mack put that thought out of his mind for the moment, concentrating on the target at hand. Rutherford would be driving a dark-blue convertible, license plate "DIAMONDS," *No shit!* Mack thought. Rutherford was often seen in the company of beautiful women, with one woman in particular.

Mack flipped through the other photos in the package, stopping on a picture of the beautiful blonde sitting next to Rutherford in the convertible. *"Carrie Falcone, age 27, nickname Candy."* Perhaps Carrie Falcone was not her real name either, but that didn't matter. She was not the intended target. He would try to keep her out of the hit, but no promises. If she got in the way, she would have to be eliminated.

Rutherford would be staying at the Blue Ocean Palms Resort, next door to Mack's hotel. Mack would be able to enter and exit the hotel from either the street side or the beach. He took up a position between the beach and the hotel that provided an excellent view of both. He then waited and watched.

As time passed, Mack began to wonder if he had missed them leaving the hotel. Walking around the back of the hotel he spotted Rutherford and Candy heading towards the beach. Mack kept his distance to make sure they would not recognize him. Rutherford was wearing red swimming trunks with a white tank top. His tanned body was adorned with gold chains and several diamond rings. He was wearing dark sunglasses with small gold lettering on the temples. Candy was dressed in a long, white, short-sleeved shirt. Mack could see the outline of a black bikini peeking out from underneath.

Picking a spot near the water, Candy dropped two beach towels. She then removed her white shirt, drawing the attention of every man on the beach. One young man's gaze followed Candy's movements across the beach and into the water. The young man's girlfriend did not seem at all pleased. Not close enough to hear the conversation between the young couple, Mack caught only the gist of it. The young girl's voice was angry. She picked up her towel and stormed off the beach. Mack heard the young man call after her, "C'mon, honey …she is not as beautiful as you." As she walked past Mack, he heard her muttering, "Bastard!" under her breath. Mack laughed to himself. *If you're going to bikini watch at the beach with your girlfriend, you need to be discrete.*

Mack watched as Rutherford and Candy swam far beyond the waves, several hundred yards from the beach. Mack walked to the edge of the water to get a better view. He could tell that Candy was a much more accomplished swimmer as Rutherford appeared to be struggling with each stroke. A plan formulated in Mack's mind. The sun was starting to set when Rutherford and Candy made their way back to the beach. Mack returned to his position between the beach and the hotel. As they got closer to the beach, Rutherford clung to Candy, holding on until they got into shallow water.

"Howie, you all right?"

"It's just my asthma acting up. I'll be okay in a moment," Rutherford said gasping for air with each word.

The loving couple dried themselves off, put on their shirts and walked back to their hotel.

Mack followed at a short distance. Rutherford and Candy entered the hotel elevator stopping at floor 11. Mack pushed the down button to see if the elevator would return immediately. Within a few moments, it arrived at the lobby.

Mack returned to his room and opened the door to the balcony. According to Rippy, Rutherford's room should be visible from his location. Mack saw Rutherford and Candy sitting on sand-colored lounge chairs. Candy moved the back of the lounge chair into the prone position, removed her bikini top and laid on her stomach. The sun, though officially set for the day, provided enough ambient light for Mack to see clearly. It would be dark soon, so Mack quickly obtained his spotting scope and sonic microphone that Rippy provided. He picked up the device and put the earphones on his head. The device contained only two switches, an on/off and volume control. Mack turned it on and set the volume to half way.

Mack turned out the lights in his room. Sitting in the shadows, he felt at home. Looking through his spotting scope, he first picked up voices with an Asian accent. Adjusting the device slightly, he heard Rutherford.

"Yeah, babe, if I keep swimming like that, I'll be in shape in no time. And if you keep doing that 'skinny dippin', I may never leave the water."

"Maybe I should keep my bikini on, you almost didn't make it back to the beach. Maybe we shouldn't go out so far."

"Forget that, if you skinny dip any closer to the beach, the whole world will get to see your hot body. I'm not sharing that view with anyone," Rutherford said, his voice throaty with excitement.

"Same time tomorrow then?"

"Wouldn't miss if for all the diamonds in the world," Rutherford spouted.

This would be the perfect opportunity to strike. Checking the phone book in his room, he found a small business that rented boats and scuba gear and then called in a reservation. *If all goes as planned, Rutherford will have a swimming lesson tomorrow, one that he won't survive.*

Mack listened to Rutherford and Candy for a while longer but soon tired of their trivial conversations. Nice weather, possible vacations in Aruba, Jamaica, the Virgin Islands. After complaining about the mosquitoes, Rutherford got up and entered his room.

Candy sat up and put her bikini top back on. Mack watched as Candy covered her naked torso. He thought how truly beautiful she was. He had not felt this way in a long time. He could not afford to get emotionally attached. Having those feelings could cause him to hesitate, or worse, make a mistake that gets him caught.

Mack fell asleep watching television in his room's recliner. His dreams turned to Candy. There was something very unique about that girl. He just couldn't put his finger on it. She reminded him of someone from his past. Mack looked out his patio door to see if there was any activity across the street. He was half-hoping he would catch a glance of her before he left to pick up the boat and scuba gear. No such luck, only a few early-risers walking on the beach. It was going to be a gorgeous day, not a drop of rain in sight. Mack made coffee and watched the sun slowly emerge above the water.

Mack arrived at the boat rental place just before noon. A man with straggly grey hair was standing barefoot outside the entrance in the shade of the small shingled roof covering the front entrance.

"Come to rent a boat?"

"Yep, got one reserved for noon."

"You must be Mr. Brittan. Follow me, we'll take care of the paperwork, check your scuba certification card, and get you on your way."

"Sounds good to me." Mack forgot that you need to carry certification to rent scuba equipment. He didn't have one with him, especially one in the name of Paul Brittan.

"Oh crap!" Mack said as he was faking a look through his wallet.

"What's the matter? You forget to bring money with you?"

"No, I have plenty of money. I can't find my scuba certification card. Well, I guess that I have to come back some other time once I find it. Sorry for any inconvenience." Mack reached out to shake the salesman's hand.

"I am not allowed to rent scuba gear without that certification." The man looked down at his feet and then up at Mack. "I'll tell you what, you prove to me that you know how to scuba dive, and I'll rent the equipment to you. You can bring your card back when you find it."

"I appreciate that," Mack replied. "Let's go check out that gear."

Mack followed the salesman into the building. The room contained lots of scuba tanks, regulators, wet suits, fins, masks, weight belts, and other accessories. The salesman handed Mack a tank and regulator. Mack quickly attached the regulator to the tank and tested it to make sure that it was functioning properly. At first the gauge read full, then read less than half full.

"Don't want this one," Mack said. "I would never make it back to show you my certification card."

A large grin appeared on the face of the salesman. "Good enough for me. You knew right away that the gauge was malfunctioning. Where did you learn to scuba dive?"

"U.S. Navy."

"You a Navy Seal?"

"What do you think?" Mack stared back at the man with eyes that could penetrate a person's soul.

"You got that look about you. Either a Navy Seal or Green Beret. Makes no difference to me. Real Special Forces don't go around bragging about what they are. Only the wanabees do that."

Mack noticed the ring that the salesman was wearing. It was gold and bore the symbol of the Green Berets. Mack looked at the man, then the ring, then the man. "Looks like I'm in good company."

"Well...I really can't rent you the equipment without the certification. I'd lose my license if I got caught renting equipment without checking certification."

Mack pulled out a stack of hundred dollar bills and started thumbing through them. The mission depended on getting this scuba equipment.

"You still interested in renting the boat?"

"No. The boat was just the means to get me out to the ocean to do some scuba diving."

"Why don't you just take a quick look? Wouldn't do any harm just taking a look, would it?"

"I guess not," Mack said.

The salesman gathered up the scuba gear and walked out of the office towards a row of small boats tied up to an old wooden dock. The salesman stopped next to an old green boat which had seen better days. The man gave Mack a slow nod and placed the scuba gear inside the boat.

"Not the best looking boat on the ocean, but it will get you where you need to go."

"Not trying to cross the damn ocean," Mack said with a smile. "Let's fill out the paperwork and I'll be on my way."

"I trust you. Bring everything back in one piece and we'll forget about the paperwork."

Mack pulled out five one-hundred dollar bills and handed it to the salesman. "This should cover it, eh?"

"Don't believe you need a receipt either?"

"Nope, I trust you," Mack said.

Mack decided he would anchor the boat about a mile from where Rutherford and Candy would be swimming. At that distance, the small boat would almost be invisible. He knew it would take him 45 minutes to get to the area where he would wait, underwater, for Rutherford to appear. Sundown was projected for 7:30 p.m.

One hour before sundown, Mack entered the water and headed toward Rutherford and Candy. He swam nearly all the way near the top of the surface, using his snorkel and saving his air supply. After the attack, he would swim underwater until he was far enough away that he could not possibly be seen. Mack waited just a short distance from where he would strike, just high enough out of the water to see. The sun was making its way down, casting long shadows across the beach.

Mack heard laughing and saw Candy and Rutherford heading directly towards him. He slipped below the surface of the water. Through his snorkel mask, Mack could see Candy from the neck down. Rutherford was swimming after her, his shape from under the water looked like an overweight walrus.

As Candy and Rutherford were treading water, Mack watched as Candy removed her bikini top and her bikini bottoms were soon to follow. She threw them towards Rutherford and swam away. Rutherford started swimming after her, but was having difficulty closing the distance. He would tread water for a short time, and then swim towards Candy. Each time he got close, she teasingly swam away.

Mack positioned himself directly below Rutherford. Rutherford swam a short distance again, Candy still swimming away. *Time to strike.* Grabbing one of Rutherford's legs, Mack yanked him underwater, spinning him at the same time. Mack watched as Rutherford began to panic, becoming disoriented and starting to lose consciousness. Continuing this process for about a minute, he let him go free. Rutherford's limp body floated to the surface. Mack watched for a few moments before heading back to the boat.

"Come on. If you catch me, you can have me," Candy said sheepishly.

Rutherford did not respond. Candy swam closer.

"Howie? Howie? Are you all right?"

Candy grabbed Rutherford and realized that he was not conscious.

"Help. Help. Someone please help me."

Candy was struggling to keep Rutherford and herself afloat. Her screams attracted the attention of some nearby beach-goers and a male life guard. When the lifeguard finally reached the pair, he took control of Rutherford and started making his way back to the beach.

"Can you make it back on your own?" the young tanned lifeguard asked.

"I think so."

Candy swam ahead of the lifeguard, reaching the beach first. She made it almost completely out of the water before she noticed that all the eyes on the beach were on her and ducked back under the water.

"Can someone please bring me a towel?"

A teenage boy picked up his beach towel and ran it over to Candy. She grabbed the towel from the boy and wrapped it around her naked body. Exiting the water, she found her shirt and shorts and pulled them on. Unwrapping the towel, she handed it back to the boy, who was grinning from ear to ear. He held onto it like a hard fought trophy as his buddies slapped him on the back.

By this time, the lifeguard was closing in on the beach and several good Samaritans helped him get Rutherford out of the water. The lifeguard started CPR, but Rutherford did not respond. Candy hovered as the lifeguard worked furiously, pushing on Rutherford's chest and breathing into his mouth. Shortly, an ambulance arrived and the paramedics took over. Despite the paramedics attempt to revive Rutherford, his body remained lifeless. One of the paramedics pulled out his stethoscope. He shook his head and tapped his partner. They lifted the body onto a stretcher, covered it with a blanket, and placed it in the back of the ambulance. The ambulance drove off the beach slowly, without lights or siren.

In the meantime, a local police officer was interviewing the lifeguard.

"What happened?"

"I heard screaming and saw a woman frantically waving and trying to hold someone up."

"And then what?"

"I swam out to where she was and found her trying to hold a man's head out of the water."

"What man?"

"The one that the paramedics are working on."

"Where's the woman?"

"The good-looking blonde over there," the lifeguard said pointing at Candy.

"Was the man conscious when you found him?"

"No. Once I got him to the beach I started CPR and waited for the paramedics."

The policeman jotted down some remarks in a small black notebook and walked over where Candy was sitting in the sand.

"You the person in the water with that guy they took away in the ambulance?"

"Yes. We were just swimming."

"So what happened," the policeman said suspiciously.

"We've been swimming before sunset for several days. Last night, I told him that he shouldn't go swimming with his asthma."

"You're saying he had an asthma attack?"

"Maybe. I don't know. He had a difficult time making it back to the beach yesterday. He was out of breath when we got out of the water. I told him not to go out so far, but he insisted."

"What was your relationship to him?"

"I'm his girlfriend."

"Just stay here until I get back. I'm going to talk to some of the other witnesses."

Candy sat down on the beach and waited for the officer to return.

"OK. ma'am. I spoke to some of the bystanders and they said that you got out of the water without wearing any clothing. Can you explain this?"

"It's rather embarrassing. I'd rather not explain."

"You can explain now, or you can explain down at the station."

"Sorry," Candy said as she started to cry. "I was skinny dipping. I didn't mean any harm. I was just teasing Howie."

"Who is Howie?"

"My boyfriend. The one they took in the ambulance. How is he? Is he going to be okay?"

"I don't know his condition, ma'am. Let's get back to the incident. Tell me what happened."

"Like I said, we were swimming. I took my bikini off and was teasing Howie. He liked to, you know, play around. The next thing I knew, he was floating face down. I yelled for help and the lifeguard came and pulled him to shore."

"Write your name, address, and phone number here in my notebook."

Candy did as the officer asked and handed the notebook back.

"Here is my business card. If you have any questions, you can reach me at the number listed."

"Thanks," Candy said as he picked up her beach towel and walked back to her hotel.

As planned, Mack swam back to the boat, staying underwater as much as possible. Once inside the boat, he removed his scuba gear and drove back to the marina. By the time he arrived, it was long after dark. He parked the boat in the slip where he found it and stowed the scuba gear so that it wouldn't be stolen. There was a light on in the sales room, but he decided to wait until tomorrow to return the boat.

"All finished for the day?"

Mack spun around, surprised by the salesman in the shadows.

"All finished for the week."

"So you don't need it tomorrow then?"

"Nope. I'm finished. Hadn't been scuba diving in years, so I figured what the heck. I'm on vacation and had both the time and the money. Tomorrow I might go skydiving."

"Nice doing business with you."

"Yeah," Mack replied.

The salesman turned and walked back into the office. On his way back to his hotel, Mack wondered whether the salesman would get suspicious and talk to police after news of Rutherford's death was reported. Didn't matter much, Mack had used a fake name, and the store did not have any video cameras. Also, he had wiped down the boat and scuba gear.

Mack turned on the radio and listened to the news. "Howard Rutherford, age 65, was pronounced dead by paramedics after lifeguards rescued him from the water. Based on eye-witness accounts, it appears to be an accidental drowning. Sources close to law enforcement say that Rutherford almost drowned the day before, but was saved by a female companion. Rutherford was also reported to have severe asthma and was swimming beyond a safe distance from the beach."

Mack turned off the radio. His plan had worked. His mind now turned to Candy. He decided to go to the bar after he got cleaned up and changed clothes. He was hoping that he would see her there and arrange a chance encounter to talk to her. It was becoming clear that his interest in this girl was increasing. However, there was still something that he could not put his finger on, something about her that made her stand out from other women. Perhaps if he got to know her better, he would be able to figure out what it was about her that was driving him mad.

Mack returned to his room and took a shower. While he was putting on his clothes, the cell phone that Rippy provided rang.

"Yeah, whatcha want?"

"Just got word that the work is finished. Good job. The next project is almost ready. Be prepared to leave tomorrow."

"You know how to get a hold of me," Mack stated.

"Indeed we do," Rippy said as he hung up the phone.

Pompous ass. Rippy knew where Mack was at all times. The cell phone was GPS enabled and the SUV that he was driving was similarly equipped. Mack also suspected that Rippy had some of his cronies keeping tabs on him wherever he went. This didn't bother him. When the time was right after the last job, he would disappear. He would arrange for payment prior to the last job.

He finished dressing and took the elevator down to the lobby. He decided to get a beer at the hotel bar, hoping to catch the evening news regarding Rutherford, and maybe a glimpse of Candy too. Mack walked into the bar, ordered a beer, and found an empty spot at the bar. Mack took a few swigs and listened to the other folks at the bar. The conversation of choice was the excitement caused by an accidental drowning of a tourist just yards from where they were sitting. One of the gentleman sitting at the bar turned to Mack and said, "You there this evening when some dude drowned?"

"Nah, missed it. Must have been rather exciting though."

"Actually, that wasn't all that exciting. The exciting part was when the guy's girlfriend got out the water totally naked, screaming for help. Hell, I thought someone raped her, or a shark tore off her bikini the way she was acting."

"You're shitting me....some chick got out of the water totally naked?"

"Yep, saw it with my own eyes. That girl has one hard body. Only got to see it for a second or so before she realized that she wasn't wearing any clothes. No tan lines. That is what I remember most....well, you know what I mean."

"Yeah, I know what you mean. I am sorry that I missed it."

Mack thought how truly sorry he was. Although he saw her naked body while she was in the water, he saw it from a distance and through a scuba mask.

"The naked chick I mean."

"I knew what you meant," the guy said with a large grin. "Holy shit...there she is! Well I think that is her...Pretty sure, they don't make them like that every day," the guy said looking over his shoulder.

Mack turned to see what the guy was talking about. Sure enough, Candy had entered the bar and was looking around. Dressed in a white sundress, her tan appeared even darker. The bottom of her dress was half-way up the length of her thighs, fitting snuggly around her athletic body. She was wearing a pair of black stiletto shoes and carrying a small black leather purse which she had swung over her left arm.

As luck would have it, Candy took a vacant seat directly opposite Mack. The bartender immediately went over to Candy to see what she would like to drink. She too ordered a beer. Mack smiled and thought to himself. *Hot chick that also drinks beer. Does it get any better than this?*

Mack pulled his ball cap tighter down on his head. He continued his conversation with the guy next to him, careful not to make any eye contact with Candy. Mack, however, got the feeling that she was staring at him. He made a quick scan with his eyes past Candy and onto the television playing in the upper corner of the bar. She *was* staring at him. He did another quick scan with his eyes and looked past her again and confirmed it. He wondered if she recognized him from the other day on the road into Virginia Beach.

Mack took a long sip of beer and looked in Candy's direction. However, Candy was no longer seated at the bar. He quickly looked around, hoping to find the beautiful blonde. She was no longer inside the bar.

Finishing his beer, Mack walked out of the bar and headed down towards the beach. The sounds of the waves pounded the beach with systematic precision. Out of the corner of his eye, Mack spotted movement just over a large sand dune. His instinct told him that something was not right, someone may be in trouble. Walking closer, Mack heard muffled voices. He couldn't make out what was being said, but he knew his instinct was right when he heard a woman's scream. Mack started to run towards the sound and as he crested the top of the dune, he saw three young men holding down a woman.

"Get off me you piece of shit."

"We can do this the easy way, or we can do this the hard way," said a dark haired surfer looking man.

Mack recognized a voice. It was Candy. Mack clenched his fists, anger swelling within him like a boiling tea kettle.

"Let her go," Mack demanded.

Two of the men pinning Candy to the ground immediately released her and started walking towards Mack.

"You should have minded you own business old man."

As the first man got within striking distance, Mack landed a roundhouse kick directly above the man's left knee. His leg buckled, dropping him quickly to the ground. Seeing his friend go down in a large heap, the second man rushed Mack in an effort to take him down. Mack quickly side-stepped the attempt delivering a brachial stun to the side of the man's neck incapacitating him.

"I told you to let her go," Mack said.

Seeing that his companions were not successful, the young man released the pressure holding Candy to the ground. At the same moment, Candy dug her nails into the man's face, leaving three large scratch marks across the young man's face. He screamed with pain and raised his fist to strike her. Mack struck the man on the back of his head, rendering him unconscious. His limp body fell back on top of Candy.

"Get off of me," Candy said pushing the man off of her.

"You okay?" Mack said reaching out his hand.

"I am now."

Mack pulled Candy to her feet. She immediately embraced him, her trembling body held tightly against his.

"You sure you're okay? You're shaking like a leaf."

"Thank God you came along. I was walking along the beach when these guys came from behind and drug me behind that sand dune."

"You're safe now. Let's go back to the hotel. We can call the police from there."

"No more police," Candy said. "I'm fine. Today has been a horrible day. My friend drowned." The tears began to swell in Candy's eyes.

"Come on. Let's go get a drink. You can tell me all about it."

Mack escorted Candy back to the hotel bar. He ordered two beers and sat with Candy in one of the booths that lined the clubroom walls.

"Here ya go."

"Thanks. How did you know what kind I liked?"

"I saw you drinking one earlier."

"Oh my God. In all the excitement, I didn't get a chance to introduce myself. My name is Candy, what's your name?"

"Paul, Paul Brittan."

"Nice to meet you Paul. Oh my, I'm so sorry. I haven't even thanked you for rescuing me. I don't know what I would have done if you hadn't come along." The tears started flowing again.

"It's all over now. Those guys aren't going to bother anyone. Besides, you handled yourself very well. That guy will have a permanent reminder every time he looks in the mirror."

Candy wiped her eyes with a bar napkin. Mack noticed how beautifully her blue eyes sparkled.

"Are you vacationing here in Virginia Beach?" Candy said regaining her composure.

"Yeah, down here for a short period. What about you? You on vacation here too?"

"Yeah, well no, well sort of...I came down here with a guy and he accidentally drowned today...I am still shook up over it."

"Drowned? I heard something on the news. My God, what happened?"

"We went swimming in the ocean, and were having a good time. Next thing I know, Howie is face down in the water." Candy's voice changed to a more solemn tone. "Somehow, I blame myself. I told him not to go swimming again."

"How is any of this your fault? It was an accident, right?"

"That's what the police told me just a few moments ago. That is why I left the bar earlier. The death is being ruled an accidental drowning. They asked me what I wanted done with the body." Candy started to cry and Mack placed his hand on her shoulder.

"It'll be O.K. Were you engaged to him?"

"No...No...I was...uh...I was...well, I was more of eye candy for him than anything else...no pun intended."

Mack smiled at her and she returned it with a faint smile of her own.

"Howie liked the best things in life. Fast cars, large estates, and beautiful women. I guess I fit the last category."

"I would agree with that," Mack said. Candy gave Mack another faint smile.

"I don't know what to do. I can't just leave Howie here. I guess I can call Howie's friend Daniel and maybe he can help me. I just feel so helpless at this point."

"Understandable," Mack said. "Who wouldn't? If I were you, I would call this Daniel guy and let him handle everything. I'm sure he knows what to do."

"Thank you for being so kind. I just need to be with someone tonight. I don't think I can stand being in that hotel room all by myself."

Candy placed her hand on Mack's leg. The idea of taking her up to her room and spending the night in total bliss crossed his mind. However, it would not be a good idea to be seen in the room of the girl the same night that her "boyfriend" drowned. That same thought came back. There is something about this girl that he couldn't put his finger on. Something not quite right. Mack's instincts took over. He would make an excuse as to why he couldn't spend the night with her.

"I wish I could. I really wish I could," Mack said.

"Are you sure that you can't?"

"Trust me. I really wish I could."

"You don't know what you'd be missing," Candy said.

"Oh, I know exactly what I'd be missing," Mack said. "It wouldn't be appropriate given all that happened today, the drowning and all."

Candy removed her hand from Mack's thigh.

"I am so sorry. You must think I am some kind of monster. My boyfriend just drowned and I am making a pass at you. I am so sorry. I have never acted like this before." The tears welled in her eyes.

Candy pulled a pen from her purse, wrote down her cell phone number and handed it to Mack. "Call me sometime. Please?" Candy said as she turned and walked out of the bar.

- - -

"What the hell was that?" Candy shouted into the phone. "I thought you said they were just going to rough me up a bit. Those three guys just about raped me."

"We had to make it look realistic," Rippy said. "Anything short of that and he would have gotten suspicious."

"Bad enough that I had to put up with Rutherford's perverted ways. A few minutes more and those pieces of shit would have raped me."

"Well they didn't. Besides, you got your licks in too. They fared far worse than you. You need to act like the professional you are. Do what you're told," Rippy said as he hung up the phone.

- - -

Something is wrong. Mack's intuition was telling him that this girl was somehow involved in the overall operation. Way too many coincidences, the meeting on the road into town, the hotel rooms directly across the street from each other, and the final clue, the meeting at the hotel bar. Mack was sure of it now. This girl was definitely involved somehow. She was probably one of Rippy's Raiders. *That's it. That's it. That's the missing piece.* The girl was an operative. No matter how hard someone tried to hide it, there are subtle clues that a trained operative can spot. The way they say their undercover name, their reaction when they hear someone say their real name, the eye contact or lack of eye contact when not telling the truth. The slight pause before answering a question about their undercover identity, and other clues.

Mack was trained in detecting if someone is lying by using visual accessory clues, a process of watching someone's eyes to see which direction they look when answering a question. A person's subconscious causes the eyes to look in a particular direction, left, right, up, down, etcetera when either remembering a true fact or when constructing a falsity. There were other factors such as stress on speech patterns, voice inflections, little or no body movement when someone is not telling the truth. Repeated blinking, scratching, touching the nose, fidgeting, swallowing, or omitting a piece of information from an otherwise truthful statement. Trained operatives can suppress almost all of these tell-tale signs. Candy was obviously trained in these areas. She was good, but Mack's intuition betrayed Candy's deception. *Trust your instinct, not your desires.* The phrase resounded in Mack's mind like church bells ringing on a cold Sunday morning.

All of these facts had added up to one thing. Candy was not whom she appeared to be. Candy had to be involved with Rippy and this whole operation. There was no other logical conclusion. He needed to be absolutely sure. Distrust of Rippy began to creep into his mind like a drop of ink in a glass of water. While he didn't trust Rippy from the start, he had trusted that Rippy was concerned about the elimination of the twelve targets and keeping Mack from detection by the authorities furthered that purpose. However, once all twelve targets had been eliminated, Mack would be a huge liability to Rippy. If Candy knew too much, she would not be around long either.

Mack decided that he would call Candy and tell her that he changed his mind. He did want to be with her. His primary reason for reaching out was to retrieve information, *but a little romance would be an added bonus.* He had never slept with a woman to gain information, it was usually the other way around. Women try sex as an enticement to gain intelligence and often have great success. This part of the mission, Mack would enjoy. *Turn around is fair play in love and war.*

Mack pulled out the bar napkin with Candy's phone number and entered the number into the cell phone that Rippy had provided to him. After three rings, Mack started to hang up. He didn't want to leave a message. On the fourth ring, Candy answered.

"Hello?"

"Hey, this is Paul. You hanging in there?"

"Yeah, Yeah, I'm fine. How are you?" Candy's voice was soft and sweet. "Something wrong, Paul?"

"No, just the opposite. Everything is right," Mack said softly with the best tone of voice he could muster. "I've been thinking about what you said…don't know what I'll be missing. I've been thinking about you ever since you left the bar." Mack wasn't lying, he had been thinking about her.

"Me too. Are you still at the bar?"

"No, I went back to my room. If you're still up to it, I'd like to continue where we left off."

"I'd like that too. You want to come over to my room for a

drink?"

"Well, as I said before, it wouldn't look right. How about coming over to my room? I'll get some beer and food from the bar downstairs...unless you think I'm being too forward or something."

"Sounds wonderful!" Candy said. "Are you staying in the same hotel as the bar?"

"Yeah, I'm in room number 1157. I'll meet you in the bar in....let's say 20 minutes? We can have a drink and take the food and beer back to my room to watch TV, unless you would rather eat in the bar?"

"I'd rather just get the food and beer and watch TV as long as we don't watch the local news. I'm still shook up over Howie's death."

"I promise," Mack said. "No local, or national news. We can pick a movie from the On-Demand menu. A comedy might not be a bad idea. I can use a few laughs tonight."

"You pick the beer and the food, and I'll pick the movie. I'll see you downstairs in 20 minutes. See ya soon," Candy said as she hung up the phone.

Mack was smiling. It had been a long time since he had any romance. In a few short moments, he would be alone in his room with a woman who was nearly half his age and stunningly beautiful. Mack was very attractive for his age. He was in great physical shape with a very low body fat percentage. Women had been attracted to him all his life. His self-confidence and rugged good looks made him irresistible to both young and mature women.

Mack quickly put his operational gear into one of the closets and straightened out the rest of the room. Even though Candy might be one of Rippy's Raiders, and whose mission might be to hook-up with Mack, he didn't want to be embarrassed by his messy living quarters. Mack grabbed his cell phone, placed his wallet in his back pocket and took the elevator down to the lobby. A younger crowd had gathered and was dancing on the lighted dance floor. The bartender shot him a quick look and removed empty beer bottles from the bar.

"Back again? Didn't get lucky I guess?" the bartender said with a smirk on his face.

"Night ain't over yet!" Mack said with a grin.

Mack ordered some bar food and a six-pack of beer. No sooner had he paid the bartender, when Candy entered the bar. The bartender saw her first.

"Your friend is back," pointing across the bar dance floor.

"Right on time," Mack said.

"You da man," the bartender spouted.

Candy made her way over to Mack, navigating past groups of young people bumping and grinding on the dance floor. The young males were making comments that Mack couldn't hear. *Lucky for them.* Candy stopped next to Mack, leaned in close and whispered in his ear.

"You ready?"

Mack could feel her warm breath and smelled the sweet aroma of her body lotion.

"You look awesome," Mack whispered back.

Candy followed Mack across the dance floor. None of the other women in the bar held a candle compared to her. As they entered the elevator, Candy reached across Mack and pushed the button for his floor. In a few moments the elevator door opened and Candy led him out of the elevator by his hand. Mack pulled on her hand, directing her to the left towards his room. Mack slid the credit card style room key into the slot and pushed the door open, holding it open for her to enter. As he did, Candy brushed tight up against Mack, squeezing herself between the door opening and Mack. He could feel her body tight against his.

Once inside the room, Candy took the food and beer from Mack and placed it on the counter in the kitchenette. She removed two beers from the bag and opened them with the bottle opener lying next to the kitchen sink. She handed one to Mack and then took a seat on the living room couch in front of the T.V. Mack took a long swig of beer and stared at her flipping channels with the remote and taking small sips of beer. She sat on the couch with her feet spread apart and her knees together.

"I get to pick the movie right?"

"That's the deal," Mack said.

Mack could care less what movie she wanted to watch. Hell, he didn't care if it was a "chick flick". Candy was flipping through all the On-Demand channels looking for something to watch. She would start one trailer, then quickly stop and move on to the next.

"Having any luck?" Mack said from the kitchen.

"Nah, nothing so far. We'll have to pick one out together. Any suggestions?"

"No suggestions," Mack said laughing. "The movie was your part, remember?"

Candy had navigated her way to the adult section. "Howie would sit for hours watching these trailers. He sure played the part."

"Played the part? What are you talking about?"

"Howie was impotent. We were never intimate. He didn't want anyone to know that he wasn't fully, uh, uh, functional. You know what I mean," Candy said without looking at Mack.

"I get your drift," Mack said. "I'm confused, but I get your drift."

"Howie used women, like myself, to make others think that he could perform. He was extremely vain and told me that he would rather die than have the world find out that the 'King of Bling' couldn't get it up."

"So you're relationship with him was purely Platonic?"

"Purely," Candy said. "I mean, we went skinny dippy a couple of time. In fact, we were skinning dipping when he drowned. Well…at least I was skinny dipping."

"So why were you with him then?"

"I was being blackmailed. He approached me at a mutual friend's party and asked me if I'd be willing to be one of his posse. I told him no. He told me that my brother Adam owed him a lot of money. Adam has a big gambling problem. He assured me that no sex would be involved, but nudity might be required. All that I had to do was to make others think that I was his girlfriend and that he was sleeping with me. He said if I cooperated, he would erase Adams debt. It has been six months now, and he still says that the debt isn't clear."

"He's gone now. The debt should be cleared. You're free."

"I wish. Adam owed a lot of money to organized crime. They beat him up badly a couple of times when he didn't pay. Now, I don't know what to do."

"Maybe I can help. Not sure what I can do yet, but maybe."

Candy looked at Mack and smiled widely.

"That means a lot to me. Come, sit here with me."

Mack crossed the room and sat down on the couch next to her. Candy removed the beer from Mack's hand and sat it on the coffee table in front of the television. She leaned in close and kissed Mack. Her body was pressed hard against him and Mack could feel her soft hair on the side of his face. He felt a tingling sensation throughout his body that he had not felt before. He had been with women before, but never experienced this unique sensation. Candy stood up taking Mack by the hand and led him into the bedroom. Candy slid off her white body suit and stood in front of Mack totally naked. Mack closed the bedroom door and dimmed the lights.

CHAPTER SEVEN

Monongahela National Forest
Elkins, West Virginia
26 November
Day Before the Opening of Deer Season

Mack arrived in Elkins in the early morning hours. It has been snowing for a few days now with more than twelve inches lying on the ground. Elkins was an old town, once thriving from the timber and coal industries. Modern day Elkins boasted a few large retail establishments and the biggest employer was a flooring manufacturer. For the most part, ten minutes out of town was extremely rural, the landscape virtually unchanged for the past one hundred years. The snow covered mountains and the stout evergreen trees made for a scene worthy of a holiday Christmas card. It was peaceful, quiet and serene. The moonlight made the snow glow bright and the frigid temperatures were a reminder of Mother Nature's dominance in this part of the world.

Mack was driving a four-wheel-drive pickup, dressed in a camouflage jacket and pants, and wearing a blaze orange hunting cap. At this time of the year, Elkins would be crawling with hundreds of hunters, ready to challenge the forest, and the weather, for an opportunity to bag a deer. Mack was not a sportsman hunter. In fact, Mack disliked the killing of animals. It was easy for him to kill a human, someone who had committed terrible crimes or deeds and deserved to die. Most animals don't have a chance to survive given the modern day rifles, long-range optics, and a shrinking habitat to hide or escape into.

Mack didn't begrudge the sportsman for hunting, but it wasn't something that Mack would never engage in. Mack dressed in hunting clothes to blend with the hunters that would be combing the forest in search of their prey. He had also grown a scraggly beard and mustache to further hide his facial features and aid in his disguise. His beard itched. He hadn't grown one for more than twenty years. He couldn't wait to end this mission and shave it off. With luck, he would be able to eliminate the target on the first day of deer season.

Mack received the target list three days prior to his arrival in Elkins. The termination notice identified the target as *Alan Shane Samuels*, who was "*Selected for termination for crimes against the United States including sedition; terrorism; conspiracy and treason.*" Beyond that, there were no specifics about Samuels' crimes. No matter. The civilian leadership determined the objectives and left it up to the military to develop strategy and tactics to achieve them. Mack was a soldier through and through. He received orders and carried them out. He wasn't one for politics or politicians. Most politicians would say or promise almost anything to get elected and then renege on those promises once in office. Mack, along with a growing number of Americans, were disgusted with the current state of affairs including the economy. Too much liberal influence in the running of the country. Large amounts of deficit run-up to provide programs and services to non-working citizens or illegal aliens.

Mack wasn't crazy about the conservative agenda when they were in power either. Two wars, thousands of troops killed, and the nation being drained of its resources to remain a world dominant influence. Mack laughed to himself. Here was a government spending billions of dollars providing healthcare to all of it citizens and offering citizenship to millions of illegal aliens. At the same time, they were using him to assassinate twelve of its highest priority targets. The American public got a good insight into these polar opposites during the Wiki leaks episodes. *Maybe I should keep a record of all the targets and then leak them to the news media at a time and place to my advantage.* Mack dismissed the idea; he had no intention of becoming the most hunted fugitive in U.S. history. The government has a way of using scapegoats to take the blame for their own dark actions or misgivings.

Mack checked into the hotel at the edge of town. Once inside his room, Mack opened his rifle case. According to the dossier, Samuels was in Elkins to go deer hunting. He had been making the same trek for ten years, hunting in the Monongahela National Forest near the town of Parsons. He would not be alone, however. Samuels and his hunting companion would most likely enter the forest together, but then split up, each going to a different location to hunt.

Samuels would be driving a dark grey, 4x4 pickup truck with a matching painted camper. Mack used his binoculars from his room's window to see if any vehicles matched the license plate number listed in the dossier. He found the vehicle parked several spots down from his own. He didn't bother undressing; he would be asleep for only a couple of hours at most.

More than an hour had passed while Mack watched the parking lot. Several people had left the hotel, each dressed in hunting attire and carrying their firearms. Then both turn signals on Samuels' truck flashed. Mack spotted two men, dressed in hunting attire, decorated with blaze orange vests and matching color hats, approaching the truck. Quickly grabbing his gun case and backpack, he made his way to the parking lot. He slowly walked past the two men loading their gear into the truck. Mack was easily able to recognize Alan Shane Samuels, even though dressed in camouflage hunting attire.

"Good luck!" Mack said noticing the ring on Samuel's left hand as he was loading his gear into the truck. It had the same symbol as the rings the prior two targets had worn. He didn't know if Osterman had worn a similar ring, but now the coincidences were adding up.

"Same to you," Samuels said.

Mack was taken back for a second. Samuels spoke with a heavy accent.

"I'll need all the luck that I can get," Mack said over his shoulder as he was walking away, hiding his face from view.

"I've been lucky so far. If my luck holds out, I'll be returning with a trophy buck this year too," Samuels said.

There was no mistaking it. Samuels spoke with a heavy German accent. It didn't matter what nationality, but it struck him as odd that this target would be of German descent. Then there was that ring. Two individuals wearing a ring with the same unique symbol was high odds in itself, but both of them targets for elimination? Now, a third target wearing the same ring with the unique symbol? The odds were off the scale. Rutherford's death was ruled an accident. Muhler's death was considered suicide, and Osterman's was never reported to the authorities as far as Mack could tell.

Mack jumped in his truck and started the engine. Samuels and his male companion were busy cleaning off the snow that had accumulated since their arrival. Mack looked at the outdoor thermometer display in his vehicle. Seventeen degrees. Bitter cold. The sun would be coming up in an hour or so, but the day-time temperature was not expected to rise much. The night sky was clear, the stars like pinholes of light shining through an artist's black canvas.

As Mack drove across the parking lot, he could hear the snow and ice crunching under the tires. The streets in Elkins were shining in spots where the snow had melted and ice had formed. Mack had a good idea which way Samuels was heading. Elkins was a small town with all the major roadways heading out in different directions. As predicted, Samuels took the road out of Elkins heading north to the town of Parsons. Mack followed at a safe distance, just far enough behind not to raise Samuels' suspicion that he was being followed. There was only one major road leading to Parsons. It was common for vehicles to follow each other during the entire twenty mile journey.

Following Samuels up the mountain road, he noticed the steep drop off on the side of the roadway. Large portions of the road did not contain guardrails. Mack considered pushing Samuels, and his vehicle, down over the side. However, if Samuels was not killed he might be suspicious enough to hide, making it difficult to find and eliminate him. Mack dismissed the idea for now. He would stick with his initial plan.

Mack followed Samuels' vehicle without his headlights, able to see clearly from the moonlight. As they approached the town of Parsons, Mack turned his lights back on. Once through town, Samuels turned off onto a dirt road leading into the National Forest. Mack followed the vehicle down the dirt road for three miles until Samuels pulled off to the side where a place had been carved out of the forest. Mack stopped his vehicle quickly. *Did he see me? Is he pulling over to allow me to pass by?* Mack quickly backed his truck up the road and into a small trail just wide enough to fit his vehicle. He waited and watched intently. He could see the brake lights were lit on Samuels' truck. In a few moments, the brake light went out, but the vehicle didn't move. The interior lights of the truck came on as Samuels, and his companion, exited the vehicle simultaneously. Mack watched as they pulled their firearms out of their protective covers.

As they started walking into the forest, Mack grabbed his rifle from the back seat of the truck. He walked to where Samuels exited his truck and looked at the fresh footprints in the snow, paying attention to the tread pattern of Samuels' hunting boots. He walked around the other side of the vehicle and examined the footprint made by Samuels' companion. The footprints were not the same size or tread pattern. Now Mack could easily distinguish the path made by Samuels if the two men split up.

At the point where Samuels entered the forest, Mack quickly spotted footprints. Continuing on, he came across the familiar smell of tobacco smoke. The area deep into the woods was much darker, the large pine trees blocking out most of the moonlight. The sun was trying to overtake the darkness as it struggled to raise itself from the horizon, providing a small amount of light with each passing minute. Mack noticed that the footprints converged and were pointing in numerous directions. A cigarette butt near one of the footprints was still spewing a small amount of smoke. Two sets of tracks were now leading away from this area.

The predawn light was now allowing Mack to leave Samuels' trail and follow him on a parallel course. He quickened his pace to close the distance between himself and the target. Mack moved quickly through the woods, cautious not to step on any limbs or branches lying on the ground. After five minutes, Samuels came into view, walking casually down the forest path, smoking a cigarette. *This guy is an idiot!*

Samuels stooped down to pick something from the forest floor. Mack looked through the rifle scope and saw that Samuels picked up a set of deer antlers. Samuels took off his backpack and tied the antlers to the top of his pack. Samuels slung the backpack onto his body and pulled out another cigarette from his jacket pocket. As Samuels lit his cigarette, the flame from the lighter made his face glow with an eerie orange color.

Samuels took a final drag off his cigarette and threw it on the ground. He stood up from the fallen log and continued walking down the snow covered forest trail. After walking several hundred yards, the trail opened into a large clearing, bordered by steep hills on either side. Samuels found a place in the clearing where several large boulders protruded up from the ground.

Mack, noticing that Samuels had stopped in the middle of the clearing, made his way up the steep slope on the north side of the clearing. His wanted a clear view of Samuels and concealment for his escape. Mack crouched down behind a large fallen tree, using it as both camouflage and support for his rifle.

The sun had not yet risen, still several minutes before sunrise and the official start of deer season. Mack calculated the distance between his position and Samuels and dialed the distance into his rifle scope. He watched the small branches at the edge of the clearing for wind speed and direction. Mack had a clear shot at Samuels, almost impossible to miss at this distance. He decided that he would wait a few more minutes until sunrise. A rifle shot before sunrise would certainly alert any Ranger in the area.

Samuels still had the deer antlers tied to his backpack. *What an idiot!* Mack thought. Mack raised the rifle into position and placed the crosshairs of the rifle scope in the middle of Samuels' chest. Mack took a deep breath, slowing his heart beat in preparation for the shot. He started to slowly squeeze the trigger. Samuels' body get rigid and then immediately went limp. He then fell off the large boulder.

Mack was taken back for a second. Mack opened the bolt on his rifle exposing the unfired cartridge still in the breech of the gun. Mack took the round out of his rifle and pulled out a pair of binoculars. In case anyone was looking for the shooter, Mack didn't want to be seen looking through the rifle scope. Looking through the binoculars, Mack could see a large blood stain on the chest of Samuels as he lay on the ground facing towards the sky.

Samuels' body lay lifeless on the snow covered ground. Mack could hear voices coming from above the same steep slope where he was positioned. He heard a voice saying "I got him. I got him. I shot myself a huge buck." Mack turned and saw two men dressed in camouflage making their way down the steep slope on their way to the clearing. Both men passed within several yards of Mack as they traveled down the hill. Mack was still lying down behind the fallen log and quickly removed his blaze orange hat to help conceal his location. Although he had not fired the shot that hit Samuels, it was better that he not be seen in the area.

Mack watched the two men as they entered the clearing and ran to where Samuels had been shot. As luck would have it, a Forest Service Law Enforcement Agent was patrolling the trail leading up to the clearing and one of the two men flagged the officer down.

Mack knew that more vehicles would soon be entering the area, so he picked up his gear, placed the blaze orange hat back onto his head and started back down the hill away from the clearing. Mack wanted to be far away from the scene as possible when the additional law enforcement vehicles arrived. He couldn't hear what the two men were telling the officer, but didn't want to take a chance that one, or both, try to blame the shooting on someone else.

It appeared as though his fourth target had been eliminated. Mack backtracked, reversing the route that he entered. He walked at a slightly faster pace, but careful not to run. Running away from a crime scene was a sure way of drawing attention to one's self and flight could be used in a criminal proceeding to show consciousness of guilt. Unless there were other Forest Service vehicles in the near vicinity, Mack would have sufficient time to return to his vehicle and leave the forest before additional law enforcement personnel arrived.

The sun was increasing its distance above the horizon, robbing Mack of the concealment of the shadows. He arrived at his vehicle and loaded his gear into the back seat. Mack calmly drove down the trail and out onto the main road leading back to Parsons. He turned on the radio hoping to catch some details on the shooting. As Mack drove back towards Elkins, he passed several Forest Service Law Enforcement vehicles heading towards Parsons.

It had been nearly an hour since Samuels had been shot. Mack arrived at the hotel and took his rifle, and other gear, into his room. He turned on the television and watched a brief news clip about a hunting accident that had just occurred in Parsons. The news media didn't have any details other than a person had been shot while deer hunting in the Monongahela National Forest. Mack changed out of his hunting attire, put on a pair of blue jeans, a flannel shirt and threw on a dark-green goose down jacket. Mack left the hotel and drove to the local steak house which served a buffet breakfast. Mack sat in a booth where he could see the television that hung in one of the corners of the walls.

As he sat eating his breakfast, he watched the same breaking news story about the hunting accident in Parsons. After an hour of watching the same story over and over again, Mack was finishing up his coffee and preparing to leave when a new version of the breaking news appeared on the television. The newscast described an accidental shooting that had occurred just minutes after sunrise on the first day of deer season.

The victim, a white male in his early to late 50s, was shot and killed by another hunter. Sources close to the investigation report that the victim had deer antlers tied to a backpack that he was wearing. Sources indicate that the shooting will most likely be ruled accidental and that charges against the shooter will not be filed. The news then reminded hunters to confirm their target before firing and "not to carry or place deer antlers while deer hunting otherwise risk being mistaken for a deer." Mack laughed to himself. It's a pretty sad state of affairs when the news has to remind people not to strap deer antlers to their body during hunting season. If Mack had not seen it with his own eyes, he would have not believed it.

Mack picked up the bill the waitress had left on his table and walked to the cash register. Mack handed it to a young, attractive girl working the register. One of the things that Mack noticed while staying in Elkins was that there was not a lot of young adults living or working in Elkins. Perhaps the lack of high paying jobs was to blame. As with many small towns in the U.S., the young leave seeking higher wages and a more exciting lifestyle. Mack couldn't blame them. Elkins, as beautiful as it was, didn't have the same opportunities that large cities could offer. However, there was much more to life than the hustle and bustle of the city. Mack imagined how beautiful Elkins would be in the summer time. It would almost be worth waiting out the long, cold winter to enjoy the national forest in the spring time.

No sense contemplating the possibility of spending the "golden years" of his life here, Mack thought. There were eight more targets to contend with and there still was the issue of Candy. If he was correct that Candy was an operative, he would surely be running into her very soon. Mack needed to develop a strategy to preempt Rippy's plan. His strategy would need to include Candy. Mack's thoughts were interrupted by the young cashier.

"Cash or credit?" the cashier asked.

"Cash," Mack replied as he pulled a twenty dollar bill from his front pants pocket and handed it to the young girl. "Keep the change," Mack said with a smile.

"Thanks," the cashier said returning his smile. "You coming back to see us again?" she asked.

"No," Mack said. The young girl's smile turned to a frown. "If I do come back, I'll be coming back to see *you*."

The frown turned back to a smile, this time accompanied by a slight blush. Mack gave the girl a wink and headed to his vehicle.

He turned onto the road leading north and followed it to the edge of town. Mack didn't know which way to head because he hadn't been given his new target yet. It was best to head out of town and drive to a hotel where he could await further instructions. Mack turned onto Route 219, the same road he took that early morning as he followed Samuels to the National Forest. As he climbed up the mountain roads on his way to Parsons, he thought about the possible connection that Rippy may have with the others. Four of the twelve have been eliminated. At least three of those four wore a distinctive gold ring. He didn't get close enough to see if Osterman was wearing that same golden ring, but the odds were great that Osterman also sported the same symbol on his finger. Mack recalled seeing some photographs of Osterman on the Internet when he first received the dossier on Osterman. Once he got to his hotel room, he would search for photos of Osterman, hopefully finding one showing his hands. As Mack finished that thought, the cell phone that Rippy provided him rang.

"Mack, here."

"Where are you?" Rippy said in his raspy voice.

"You know exactly where I'm at," Mack said.

"Normally you would be correct," Rippy replied. "However, we lost the GPS signal once you turned north onto Route 219."

"I'm still on 219. Why the need to keep tracking me?"

"We have a vested interest in your success, of course," Rippy said with a hint of arrogance.

"Four down, eight to go," Mack said.

"So, the latest target has been completed?"

"Of course. I'm leaving Elkins aren't I?" Mack said back with the same hint of arrogance.

"We had assumed so," Rippy said, this time without the arrogance. "We assumed that the 'accidental hunting incident' was your work."

"Actually, it really was an accidental hunting incident," Mack replied. "Doesn't matter much though … he's dead."

"Agreed," Rippy said. "The next job will not be ready for a couple of weeks. We'll be in touch when it is time."

"You want to clue me in on where this next job might be located?" Mack inquired.

"Most likely Columbia, South Carolina," Rippy said. "You're welcome to head there now or in a couple of weeks. We need time to set the wheels in motion to ensure the target is where we expect him on a certain date and time."

"Well, you know where you can find me," Mack said amused.

"Indeed, we do." Rippy hung up.

CHAPTER EIGHT

Mack considered throwing the cell phone out the window of the truck. He knew Rippy could track his movements through the cell phone and most likely had a GPS tracker on the vehicle he was driving as well. "South Carolina?" Mack said out loud. If there was one thing for sure, Mack was making his way around the country.

Mack's thoughts turned to Candy. He wondered what she was doing at the moment. Mack wondered how many men Candy had seduced in her undercover capacity. What did it matter? Mack thought. Who cares? Mack wasn't kidding anyone. He cared. He cared a lot. Mack tried to rationalize his infatuation with Candy. She was what Mack called a triple threat. Beauty, brains, and personality. She had it all. Mack had dated plenty of beautiful women before. He had also dated a few women who could come close to his intellectual ability. He had dated a few who had a great personality and modest looks. This was the first women he became intimate with that had all three qualities.

His voice of reason was trying to warn him that getting emotionally attached to this girl could be his downfall. Mack always listened to his voice of reason. It had saved him on more than one occasion. This time, it was not as loud, nor as firm as it had once been. It was also telling him that there was something good about Candy. Something honorable. Something worthy. The one night they spent together in Virginia Beach was extremely peaceful. He had not slept that soundly in many years. *Thank God she wasn't an assassin.* If he was right, and she was honorable and worthy, he might be able to win her trust and turn the tables on Rippy. If she wasn't, then he would deal with her accordingly.

He thought about stopping along the way and calling Candy from a pay phone. That's if he could find one. He couldn't remember the last time that he saw a telephone booth. He didn't want Rippy to know that he was calling her, but he was sure to find out. With not much to lose at this point, he picked up the cell phone that Rippy provided and scrolled through the previously dialed telephone numbers until he came across the number he recognized. He dialed the number and let it ring one time before hanging up. That one ring was long enough to produce a missed call message on Candy's phone. If Candy was interested in talking to Mack, she would be returning his call in very short order. He would be able to tell from her voice whether it contained true emotions or ones created to continue the illusion. Within a few short moments, the phone rang.

"Paul? Is that you?"

"Hey girl. How have you been?" Mack said in a soft voice.

"Great. I've been hoping you would call me. In fact, I've been thinking about you every day since we last saw each other in Virginia Beach. Where are you?"

"I'm in Maryland," Mack said. "On my way to South Carolina."

"Oh my God!" Candy said with child-like speech. "I'm in Maryland too. I'm in Frederick. Are you going past Frederick? Please tell me you are."

"Sure, I can stop by there on my way to South Carolina. That's if you want to see me again," Mack said teasingly.

"Of course I want to see you again. I'm staying in a hotel here. Hang on....let me find the address. How long will it take you to get here?"

Mack thought for a second. He wasn't in Maryland yet. He

didn't want to tell Candy that he was still in West Virginia. He didn't know how much Candy knew about his mission. It was possible that she knew very little.

"I don't know. Maybe four or five hours depending on whether I stop to get something to eat or not," Mack replied.

"Don't eat...I mean please don't stop to eat. I haven't eaten yet today and we can go out for something. I know a great place that serves steak and lobster. My treat."

"How could I refuse an offer like that? I should be there in about three hours."

"I can't wait," Candy said.

Mack found himself smiling as he hung up the phone. He knew that Rippy was sure to have intercepted the call. It would be unwise for Rippy not to do so. He didn't care. Rippy knew where Candy was and he also knew Mack's location. For some reason, Rippy wanted Mack to develop an intimate relationship with Candy. That was just fine with him.

Cresting the top of the mountain, he drove past the windmill farm located on either side of the road. The large, three-bladed windmills churned slowly, generating electrical power derived from the mountain top breezes. Mack pulled to the side of the road at a spot directly across from one of the massive windmills. He rolled down his window and listened to the whooshing sound caused by the large propeller blade. He could be in Frederick in less than two hours. Candy was expecting him to arrive in three hours.

Mack thought about driving to Candy's hotel and conducting surveillance for an hour, but decided against it. Rippy would surely know that he was at the hotel and most likely had operatives watching the hotel for Mack's arrival. When the time came, Mack would need a way to avoid being tracked by Rippy.

Mack sat at the windmill farm for nearly an hour before heading out. It must drive Rippy crazy trying to figure out why he had stopped at this location, Mack thought. He would continue to do things out of the ordinary to cause Rippy concern. He would still be predictable, however. When the time came, Mack would use that to his advantage. He would have one opportunity to surprise Rippy with an inconsistent action. He would use that opportunity wisely. He knew that at some point near the end of the mission, he would have to either eliminate Rippy or make Rippy believe that he had been killed. Another option would be to eliminate Rippy and make his followers believe that Mack had been killed. Mack's choice would depend on his relationship with Candy.

If he could be assured that Candy would not betray him, he could turn Candy into a double-agent. He could utilize Candy to gather information about Rippy's master plan. He needed to be absolutely sure about her loyalty before providing her any information about his mission. The next few days spent with Candy would determine his future plans.

It was highly likely that Candy's hotel would be under surveillance. It was also likely that her room would be watched by audio and video equipment strategically hidden within the room. It was also highly likely that the individuals conducting the surveillance would be located in an adjacent hotel room on in close proximity. Video surveillance equipment emitted certain electronic signals during operations. With the right equipment, he could detect whether electronic signals were present in Candy's hotel room.

Mack arrived in Frederick ahead of schedule. He located the

hotel but did not drive into the parking lot. He drove past the hotel taking notice of the number and types of vehicles in the parking lot and in the surrounding area. The parking lot was nearly empty. Mack drove around the immediate area looking for parked vehicles with occupants still inside. He spotted two vehicles in close proximity to the hotel. One vehicle was parked along the street with a good view of the north and east side and another vehicle was within line-of-sight to the south and west portion of the parking lot. Both vehicles contained a single occupant. It was highly irregular that an occupant would be inside either of these vehicles.

Mack drove to a grocery store located within a short distance of the hotel. His route to the store was planned to make it appear as though he was stopping for food instead of conducting surveillance in the area near the hotel. Mack parked his vehicle and walked into the store. Picking up a shopping basket, he proceeded past the cash registers and into an aisle which had a view of the grocery store parking lot. Mack pretended to look at grocery items while simultaneously looking out the store's windows. He noticed one of the vehicles he spotted near the hotel pull into the grocery store's parking lot. The vehicle parked several rows down from him. Mack walked to the far end of the aisle, away from the entrance of the grocery store.

Mack needed to continue to play the part of his alias. He paid for the items using the credit card containing the name of Paul Brittan and walked out to his vehicle. Putting on his sunglasses, he searched the parking lot for the surveillance vehicle without turning his head. The vehicle was still in the same spot. Mack drove past the vehicle on his way out and noticed the occupant slumped lower into the driver's seat. It was too late. Mack had seen the man. Evidently, Rippy was still keeping Mack under surveillance. *No matter.* At this point in the overall mission, it didn't matter if Rippy knew Mack's whereabouts.

Mack turned his attention back to Candy's hotel room. He needed to check the room carefully for any hidden cameras or microphones. The cameras would surely be placed in the living room and probably the bedroom. It was unlikely that cameras would be placed inside of the bathroom, but he would conduct a sweep of that area as well. Mack drove back to the hotel and parked a few rows from the front office. The outside entrances to the hotel required a hotel guest key to gain access. Mack knew the room number, 1125, and would enter the hotel from the front entrance and take the elevator up to Candy's room.

Mack walked across the lobby and found the elevator near the front desk. A young woman was working the front desk and gave Mack a smile as he walked past her. Mack returned the smile and continued walking to the elevator. He was carrying the beer, wine and roses that he bought at the grocery store. As he approached the elevator, the door opened and a man exited. Mack could tell by the way that he walked that he was carrying a concealed weapon. He also noticed the man walked with a sense of authority and arrogance. Guns often gave people a false sense of security. In order for a weapon to be effective, one must be able to get to it quickly and use it without hesitation. Most people will not fire a weapon unless it is a life or death situation. This hesitation could easily cost them their life when dealing with a professional assassin.

Mack continued into the elevator, brushing aside any concern he had for the man with the concealed weapon. Mack pushed the "eleven" button, and as the elevator doors closed, he started to scan the elevator for a video camera. In the top left-hand corner of the elevator, Mack noticed a dome-shaped object containing a camera lens. Mack tilted his head slightly downward to make it more difficult for the video camera to obtain any footage. The elevator slowed and stopped on the eleventh floor.

Room 1125 was the third room down the corridor on his right. Mack spotted the exit sign at the end of the hallway. He stopped in front of Candy's door and listened closely, but couldn't hear any noise coming from inside the room. He walked farther down the hallway and stopped at room 1123. There he heard voices, but could not make out what they were saying. Mack then heard the distinctive chirp of a hand held radio. It was very likely that some of Rippy's raiders were set up in the adjoining room. Mack turned and walked the short distance back Candy's room. This time he knocked softly on the door. The light shining through the peep hole in the door went dim.

"Who is it?" Candy asked.

"Room service."

"I didn't order any room service," Candy said hesitantly.

"Well someone did," Mack said in a disguised voice.

"You must be mistaken," Candy said.

"I'll just leave it by the door, ma'am," Mack said trying to hold back his laughter.

Mack placed the beer and the wine at the threshold of the door and took a few steps back. The door opened slightly and Candy noticed the items lying on the floor just outside her door. She peeked her head outside of the door, first looking to her right and then turning and looking to the left. As she did, she immediately saw Mack standing in the hallway, holding the flowers and smiling widely.

"Paul. Oh my God." Candy rushed to greet Mack and nearly knocked him down, embracing him, and kissing him passionately on his lips.

"Wow," Mack said. "That sure is some kind of greeting. Did you miss me?"

Candy embraced Mack even tighter and kissed him more passionately.

"How's that for an answer?" Candy said keeping her body tight against Mack's.

"I would say you definitely missed me."

"You smell wonderful," Mack said as he placed his face next to Candy's neck.

"Are those for me?"

"Of course…the only thing more beautiful than these roses is you."

Candy blushed slightly, averting her eyes away. Mack knew immediately that Candy's feelings for him were genuine. He could tell that she was hiding something and he knew exactly what that was. Candy was an operative working for Rippy. Now, Mack had to determine how much Candy knows about his mission. He figured that she was not a seasoned operative. A seasoned operative would never get so emotionally involved with a civilian. Mack would conduct some counter-surveillance of Candy's room and enhance his relationship with her over the next several days. He would "plant a seed of doubt" in Candy's mind, causing her to question her commitment to Rippy and the overall mission. He had an uphill battle on his hands. There was no question about Mack's loyalty. However, Mack was beginning to question Rippy's motives and loyalty.

Why would Rippy introduce a female operative into the

mission? The most likely answer was to create a liability for Mack. If Mack became emotionally attached to Candy, he could use her as leverage. The other answer is to feed Rippy information on Mack's knowledge of the other pieces of the mission, the pieces that Rippy would be trying to keep secret.

"Hey? What's wrong?" Mack asked.

"Nothing…everything is great," Candy said looking into Mack's deep blue eyes. "C'mon, I'll let you buy me a beer."

Candy took Mack by the hand and led him back to her room. She placed the wine on a small wooden table just inside the entrance to the room. The room was pleasantly furnished with a kitchenette. Mack walked to the small living room and turned on the television. Candy followed close behind him and took the seat next to him on the sofa. Candy handed Mack one of the beers. Mack took a long swig of beer and placed the beer bottle down on the oak coffee table in front of him.

"Man, that hit the spot."

"There's plenty more where that came from," Candy said.

Mack leaned in closer and placed a very passionate kiss on Candy's lips.

"There's plenty more where that came from too," Mack said with a grin.

Candy returned Mack's passionate kiss pulling herself even closer, and tighter, against his body. He could feel her warm, sensuous body against his. Her soft, subtle lips rubbing his cheeks as she moved her face down to his neck. Mack felt the soft texture of her hair against his skin. Candy's perfume and body lotion smelled like wildflowers after a new fallen rain. Mack pulled back a little from Candy's embrace.

"What's wrong?" Candy asked.

"Nothing's wrong," Mack replied. "Trust me…nothing's wrong. There's nothing that I want more right now than to continue this. I just want to slow down a little and enjoy every second." Mack wasn't really telling a lie. He did want to slow down before he completely made an idiot of himself.

"Is there something that you're not telling me?" Candy asked softly. "Don't tell me that you're married."

"Of course I'm not married," Mack said acting annoyed. "Just the opposite."

"Just the opposite?" Candy inquired.

"Let's finish our beers and go out for something to eat. Any place you want to go. Your treat, remember?"

"Sounds wonderful," Candy replied as she picked up her beer and drained it with one long swallow. "Give me a minute to freshen up and I'll be ready for a night out on the town."

"Take all the time that you want. I'm not going anywhere."

Candy rose from the couch and squeezed passed Mack in the small space between him and the coffee table, giving him a wink and a smile. Mack watched her walk across the living room and into the bathroom. Once the door closed behind her, Mack removed his cell phone from his right front pants pocket. During his stay in Elkins, he found an application, or "app" for his cell phone which detected electronic signals emanating from surveillance equipment such as video cameras. The phone indicated strong electronic signals emanating from nearby electronic devices. Mack was able to distinguish between the hotel's wireless internet signal and what appeared to be video surveillance equipment.

When Mack downloaded the "app", the program stated that video signals can not only be detected, but display on the cell phone user's screen. Mack selected one of the signals and pushed the "Display Signal" button. Immediately, a black and white image of Candy's hotel room was displayed. In the center of the image, Mack saw himself sitting on the couch. The video surveillance camera must be located near the right side of the television, hidden behind an artificial palm tree. Mack selected another one of the signals and the image displayed indicated a camera located near a toaster on the kitchenette counter. Mack checked the other signals but none of them were video surveillance equipment. He wondered if Candy knew that her hotel room was under video surveillance. He needed to find out.

Mack picked up a remote control lying on the coffee table and walked to the cabinet containing the television. He barely noticed a small, black, business card sized device laying at the base of the artificial palm tree. He finished his beer and placed the empty bottle near the device, blocking the view of the camera. He then walked over to the kitchenette, grabbed another beer, popped the top, placing the bottle opener in front another identical device sitting next to a toaster. Mack grabbed his beer and returned to his seat on the couch. He picked up his cell phone and opened the program to observe the surveillance camera images. The first image now contained a very blurry, distorted image of the living room. The clear beer bottle effectively rendered that camera's image useless. Mack checked the image from the camera located near the toaster and it depicted a black screen. *Now…to sit and wait and see if Candy would move the two objects.*

In a few moments, Candy reappeared from the bathroom. She was stunningly beautiful, dressed in a grey sweater dress which accented her voluptuous figure. Around her thin waste, she wore a wide, black belt with a golden buckle. The bottom of her dress stopped just short of her knees, exposing her long, tanned legs. Her blonde hair was neatly styled and framed her face quite nicely. Candy bent slightly forward as she placed on one grey shoe, and then the other. As she did this, Candy was looking at Mack, smiling widely. Candy's smile lit up her entire face. She had an honest, trustworthy look. When she finished putting on her shoes, she grabbed her jacket and purse.

"Ready?" Candy asked.

"Almost," Mack said. "Just need to finish this beer."

"Hey, save some for me," Candy said as Mack starting tipping the beer bottle up.

Mack handed her the nearly half empty beer bottle. She took the bottle and quickly drank the remaining contents, placing the empty beer bottle in the trash can located under the sink.

"Hang on…I left an empty beer bottle over here," Mack said walking towards the beer bottle blocking the surveillance camera.

"Leave it…the maid can get it in the morning," Candy said as she held out her jacket for Mack's assistance.

Mack felt an immediate sense of relief. If Candy knew of the video surveillance cameras, she would have left Mack remove the beer bottle blocking the view. Mack helped Candy with her coat and handed her a black purse with a golden clasp that matched the golden buckle on her belt. As he handed Candy her purse, Mack placed a small, cigarette-sized device on the kitchen counter.

Mack had a wonderful dinner with Candy at a local steakhouse. He was very happy now, happier than he had been at any point in his life. The waiter brought the bill to the table and as Mack reached for it, Candy snatched it as soon as the waiter placed it on the table.

"My treat. I wouldn't think of you paying for this wonderful meal. I am so thankful that you stopped to see me. I've thought of nothing else but you since the last time we saw each other."

"You've been on my mind a great deal too," Mack said not looking at Candy. Her eyes were full of tears.

"Now I've done it. I've made you cry."

"These are not tears of sadness, Paul. These are tears of great joy and happiness," Candy said choking back more tears.

"I know that we've only know each other for a short period of time, Paul, but I think that I've fallen in love with you."

"Paul, are you okay? I'm so sorry that I told you that…I just had to say it. Please forgive me."

"No apologies. I can see how you feel just by looking in your eyes."

Candy dried her eyes with the white dinner napkin.

"There is a lot that you don't know about me though," Candy said not looking at Mack. "I'm struggling to come to grips with several issues in my life."

"I'm sure there is a lot that we don't know about each other. I would be glad to learn anything about you. If you need someone to talk to, I'm there for you," Mack said in a most sincere tone.

Candy started to cry again. "Paul, there is something that I have to tell you and it won't be easy. I'm not who you think I am," Candy said reluctantly. "I am …" Mack cut her off mid-sentence.

"Hold that thought," Mack said quickly. "I want to hear everything that you have to tell me, but this is not the place."

Candy paid the bill and Mack left the tip despite Candy's objection. Mack noticed a car following them at a distance all the way back to the hotel. He watched intently, not knowing who was following him. Mack and Candy entered the hotel lobby and took the elevator back to their room. She entered the room first and pulled two beers from the refrigerator. She opened both beers and handed one to Mack. Mack secretly picked up the device he planted and placed it in his pocket without Candy noticing.

"Well, what I wanted to tell you is…" Mack again stopped Candy in mid-sentence. It was as if she could read Mack's mind.

Candy reached out and took the beer out of Mack's hand, placing it on the counter. She drew closer to Mack and embraced him tightly, her warm body held tight against his. Mack leaned in close to Candy's ear and whispered, "There's no better place to come clean than in the shower."

"I thought you would never ask," Candy whispered back.

Candy took Mack by the hand and guided him into the bathroom. Once inside, Candy closed the door, turned on the fan and passionately kissed Mack.

"Not a soul can hear us now," Candy whispered. Candy undressed, turned on the shower and stepped inside, leading Mack by the hand.

"My real name is not Candy. It is Carrie. Carrie Falcone."

Mack's was pleased. *Maybe she's not involved in the mission.*

"Candy, or should I call you Carrie?"

"Please call me Candy. I changed it because I never liked my real name."

"I like it much better than Carrie too."

Mack led Candy out of the shower and into the bedroom without drying off. As he laid next to her, he thought about the mission and the connection that each of the targets had with Rippy. Mack was able to find a picture of Osterman on the Internet getting into a limousine. Mack zoomed in on the photograph of Osterman's left hand. *That's the same ring. Something isn't quite right here.* Mack's thoughts were interrupted by Candy's movement.

"Morning!" Candy said as she awoke. "Have you been awake for long?"

"Not long," Mack said holding Candy tightly.

"Ready for Round Two?" Candy said teasingly.

"Round Two, Three or Four."

"Well then, I better get some breakfast and increase my energy. You'd better get some breakfast too…you're going to need it," Candy said as she slid her body across Mack as she got out of bed.

Candy went into the bathroom and closed the door. Mack got out of bed and followed quickly behind.

"That was quick," Candy said.

"Wouldn't want to waste the water," Mack said as he entered the shower with Candy. Must have been exiting hanging out with Howie. You said he was in the diamond business?"

"Mostly boring, but there were times when it was rather exciting."

"Oh yeah? How exciting?" Mack said teasingly.

"Not that way silly. One time I overheard Howie talking on the phone to someone and he mentioned the 'Ring of Twelve'.

"Ring of Twelve? What the heck is that?"

"Not quite sure. I think it has something to do with an off-shore account. I heard him arguing with someone on the phone named Steiger. I think he was being squeezed to give this guy money."

"Why do you think he was being squeezed?"

"Well, Howie mentioned that he put more than enough money in the account. He wasn't going to put in anymore."

"Did it seem to bother Howie?"

"When he hung up, it seemed like he received horrible news. I asked him if he was all right, and he told me he was, but he was shaking and he was white as a ghost."

Mack finished his shower and grabbed his cell phone to display the video surveillance cameras. The obstructions had been removed. He grabbed the motion sensor activated video camera he placed on the counter earlier and downloaded the camera's video footage. The video showed two men entering the room, moving the objects, and one man searching Mack's backpack. He noticed that one of the men placed a small item into his backpack before they left the room.

Mack finished getting dressed and Candy appeared from the bathroom dressed in a pair of form fitting grey slacks and a maroon turtleneck sweater.

"Wow, you look awesome."

"Thanks, I'm glad you think so."

"What's not to like?" Mack said looking at Candy from head to toe.

"I'll be with you in a minute, babe. Just want to finish getting ready."

Mack grabbed his backpack and returned to the bedroom. He carefully opened the small side pocket and found a small disc, roughly the size of, and double the thickness, of a dime. It was black in color and had a plastic covering. *A tracking device?*

Mack reached for his cell phone and searched for a program. He found what he was looking for with an application entitled "Paranoia". The developer of the program touted its ability to detect signals emitted by tracking devices. Mack downloaded the application and turned it on. Immediately, the display indicated numerous signals emitted by tracking devices with a color graph indicating the approximate location. The display indicated that a device was near his backpack. As Mack moved the phone closer to his backpack, the signal strength meter increased. Mack already knew about this device, but the display indicated several more.

Mack located several more tracking devices in the bedroom. One in Candy's purse, another inside the lining of her coat and yet another device in a pair of black shoes that Candy often wore.

Mack accounted for every tracking device except for one. *What's the matter with this thing?* Mack held the meter close to his left shoe and the meter registered a slight increase. He then held his right shoe close to the meter and the signal strength peaked. *What the heck?* Mack turned the shoe over and examined the sole. On the edge of the front of the heel, he noticed that a small slit, almost invisible if one didn't know what they were looking for. The slit in the heel was the same size and diameter of the black, plastic tracking device. Mack pulled the slit slightly apart and saw a tracking device inside. Someone must have entered his room in Elkins while he was out tracking Samuels in the National Forest. Mack left these shoes in his room and wore hunting boots when he left the hotel.

The cell phone Rippy provided started to ring.

"Yeah, what's up?" Mack said.

"Say nothing, just listen. The next target is in Las Vegas. South Carolina will have to wait. Your mission paperwork is at the hotel front desk with the name "Paul Brittan" on it. Inside you will find instructions and several credit cards."

"Mind if I take a friend?"

"If you want to take along your woman friend, do so at your own expense," Rippy said slightly irritated.

"Thanks, I will," Mack said as he hung up the phone.

"You taking a friend somewhere?"

"Yeah, how would you like to go to Vegas?" Mack asked smiling.

"Vegas? I'd love too. When can we leave?"

"Soon, we'll make the plane reservations for tomorrow if that's all right?"

"I'll start packing," Candy said excitedly.

Mack left the room and took the elevator down to the lobby. He asked the gentleman behind the reception counter if he had a package for Paul Brittan. The gentleman reached under the counter and pulled out a large, brown envelope addressed to Paul Brittan in black, felt pen.

"There you go, sir. We didn't know what room you were in. We didn't have you registered as a guest here. A gentleman dropped this off a couple of hours ago and said that you will be stopping by to pick it up."

"Thanks," Mack said as he took the envelope from the receptionist.

"You're welcome. Hope you enjoy your stay with us," the gentleman said with a smile.

"Having the time of my life," Mack said as he walked to the elevator.

CHAPTER NINE

When Mack returned to the room, Candy was busy packing her belongings in the bedroom. Mack sat on the sofa in the living room and opened the envelope. *"Michael R. Steiger—Selected for Termination for Crimes Committed Against the United States."* Again, no specific crimes were listed. Steiger's photograph depicted a man in his late fifties or early sixties with grey hair and glasses. Standing in front of a Las Vegas casino, Steiger was wearing a dark suit and carrying a brown leather briefcase. On his left hand, he wore a large, gold ring.

Steiger. That was the name Candy said Rutherford called the other person on the phone. Steiger lived in Las Vegas and spent most of his time gambling in the casinos. Mack looked at the rest of the documents inside the envelope. One of the documents contained instructions to leave his vehicle at Baltimore-Washington International airport short-term parking and lock the keys inside the vehicle. Mack also found flight reservations and ticket information for his flight to Las Vegas the next morning. Mack called the airline and arranged for Candy to travel on the same flight. Mack upgraded his ticket to first class and Candy's ticket as well. *Rippy can afford it.* He put his shoes, which contained the tracking device, in his duffle bag. He then tossed the envelope that Rippy provided inside his backpack.

Mack and Candy's flight to Las Vegas went off without incident. They grabbed a taxi to the hotel where Rippy had arranged a room. Once inside their room, Mack called the front desk and asked if a more lavish room was available. The concierge arrived in a few minutes with keys. Mack and Candy followed the concierge onto the elevator and up to a higher floor. The concierge opened the door and allowed Mack and Candy to enter. This space was much larger than the previous room, five times larger in fact. The room had a large kitchenette with two separate bedrooms, each equipped with a large whirlpool tub, and a glass enclosed shower. The two bedrooms were identically furnished, each with a luxurious king-size bed and large flat screen televisions mounted on the wall.

"Will this suit your needs, sir?"

"Well, I guess we'll have to rough it," Mack said handing the gentleman a hundred dollar bill.

"We'll need two bottles of your best champagne."

"Certainly," the concierge replied. "I'll have it sent right up."

Mack closed the door behind the man and winked at Candy.

"C'mon, let's go to the pool. I need to work on my tan."

Mack put on a pair of black swimming trunks, a grey tank top, and a pair of sandals. Candy emerged from the bathroom wearing a white bikini which made her tan appear even darker. Candy pulled on a long T-shirt which just barely covered her bikini bottoms.

The pool was surprisingly full. Candy selected a pair of lounge chairs and carefully laid out the towels that she brought with her. Mack removed his tank top revealing his highly toned, athletic shape. Candy removed her long T-shirt and immediately drew the attention of the other sunbathers. As she sat in the lounge chair and adjusted the backrest, Mack watched the on-looker's reaction. More women than men were staring at Candy as if to find flaws with her. She had no flaws. She looked like she just walked off a fashion show runway. Mack flagged down the poolside waitress and ordered a bucket of beers. Within moments, the waitress delivered six beers in a small metal bucket full of ice. Mack opened one and handed it to Candy.

"Thanks, Paul."

Mack sat back in his lounge chair, soaking in all that desert sun. The sun felt good against his body. Candy had put her chair in the prone position and had rolled over on her stomach to tan her back. Mack picked up a magazine lying next to his lounge chair. As he started to flip through the pages, he noticed a picture of Steiger with several other gentlemen, each dressed in business suits. He recognized Steiger from the upside down "V" shaped scar on his chin, an injury from a skydiving accident a few years ago. The caption below the photograph read: "*Las Vegas Symposium for Certified Public Accountants, 2015.*" Steiger owned Steiger Accounting Group, LLC with the main office in Las Vegas and satellite offices in seven states. The dossier provided Steiger's home address and license plate numbers of his vehicles. One of Steiger's favorite hobbies, other than gambling large amounts of money at the casinos, was skydiving.

Candy rose from her pool side chair and walked to the edge of the pool. Her voluptuous figure and dark tan drew the attentions of many on-lookers. Candy sat on the edge of the pool, soaking her feet in the cool water.

"C'mon Paul. Let's go for a swim."

"Thought you'd never ask," Mack said raising out of his chair.

Mack dove into the pool and Candy followed closely behind. As they made their way to the center of the pool, Mack pulled Candy close to him and whispered in her ear. "I've got work to do. I need to head down to the casinos to see if I can locate someone."

"Can I go along?" Candy whispered back.

"Sure, if you want to."

"Ok, let's go back to the room and get showered and changed."

"Another shower?" Candy said teasingly. "How about a hot tub and a bottle of champagne?"

"Oh, I forgot all about the champagne...but I sure didn't forget about that hot tub."

As Candy exited the pool, the water made her bikini semi-transparent. Mack heard a nearby man say "Damn." Mack looked at the man and gave him a knowing wink.

Mack and Candy returned to their room, showered and started to get dressed.

"Wear something hot, babe? I want every man to be jealous."

Mack changed into black Chino pants, a grey polo shirt, and black leather shoes. He wore a black leather belt with a silver buckle. This was about as dressed up as Mack got. He put on a silver Rolex Submariner watch with a small pair of military paratrooper wings fastened to the band. He also wore a silver ring with the Green Berets insignia.

Candy emerged from the bedroom dressed in a yellow dress that hugged every curve of her body. For the first since Mack had met her, Candy had her hair pulled back into a small bun. Candy had significantly more make-up on, which further highlighted her immense beauty. She wore diamond earrings which sparkled brightly as moonlit stars. Around her neck, she wore a silver necklace with a blue sapphire surrounded by twelve diamonds. Her yellow high-heeled shoes added the finesse touch to her outfit.

"I never thought I would love yellow so much," Mack said winking at Candy.

The dossier indicated that Steiger spent nearly all of his free-time in the casino where Mack and Candy were staying. It wasn't difficult to tell where the casino floor was located, they just followed the mass of tourists to the gambling facility. The casino was like most others, the lights and sounds from all the slot machines permeated the area. Candy stopped at one of the dollar slot machines and removed a one-dollar bill from her small, yellow leather purse and placed it into the machine. She quickly pulled the handle and was soon rewarded three stars across the wheels. The slot machine rang loudly which drew the attention of other gamblers. Candy had just won one-thousand dollars on a single pull. Candy jumped up and down, smiling widely at Mack, pointing at the machine.

"Oh my god. I won. I won."

Candy pushed the ticket button on the slot machine and received a printed voucher.

"Let's go cash this in and hit the tables," Candy said leading Mack to the cashiers' cage.

The man behind the cage took the voucher and counted out ten one-hundred dollar bills. Candy picked up the money and handed it to Mack.

"Here, use this money at the gaming table."

"I have money with me." Mack pulled out two large silver money clips, each packed full of hundred-dollar bills.

Mack and Candy soon found the gaming tables. He knew that Steiger like to play Blackjack above all else, often playing a thousand dollars a hand. Mack spotted two men near the Blackjack tables, sitting at a couple of slot machines. Both men were more interested in watching Mack's direction than playing the slots. He scanned the tables and immediately recognized Steiger sitting at the middle table.

"Hi," Candy said as she sat down next to Steiger. "Is this seat taken?"

"No, please have a seat," Steiger said motioning for Candy to sit down.

Mack did not ask Steiger if his seat was taken, he just sat down next to him. Candy started small talk with Steiger. Mack pulled out one of his two silver money clips and cashed in two thousand dollars. He placed two one-hundred dollar chips on the table and the dealer dealt the cards. Candy had cashed in a hundred dollars and placed the single chip on the table and received her cards. Steiger, on the other hand, bet the table maximum of one-thousand dollars. Mack's down card was a ten of hearts. The dealer dealt Mack the Queen of Spades and Mack froze his bet. Mack didn't know what Candy's down card was, but she had a seven of clubs showing. Steiger had a five of spades as his top card. The dealer turned to Steiger and asked if he wanted another card. Steiger carefully looked at his base card, thought about it for a moment, and asked the dealer for another card. The dealer placed a jack of spades in front of Steiger, causing him to bust. Steiger turned over his cards and Mack noticed that he already had fifteen before taking another card. *Steiger is a risk taker.*

Now it was Candy's turn. Candy looked at her bottom card which was the four of diamonds. She asked Steiger for his advice. Steiger looked at her bottom card and told Candy to take another card. The dealer placed the ten of diamonds on top of Candy's cards, giving her twenty-one. The dealer turned over his card and stayed at seventeen. The dealer took Steiger's chips, and provided Mack and Candy with their winnings. Steiger had bet his last chip and asked Candy if she wanted to get a drink. Candy told Steiger that she was with her friend, Paul Brittan, and asked if it was okay to bring him along. Steiger agreed without hesitation and the three of them left the Blackjack table for the bar.

Once inside the bar, Steiger flagged down a waitress and ordered his usual, triple shot of scotch. Mack ordered a double shot of Irish whisky, and Candy ordered a frozen daiquiri. Within a few moments, the waitress bought them their drinks and Candy sucked the delicious nectar of her frozen drink slowly through the small, pink straw, savoring each taste. Steiger watched Candy intently without speaking until she broke the silence.

"So, my name is Candy and this is Paul," Candy said gesturing to Mack.

"Nice to meet you. My name is Michael Steiger, but most people just call me Steiger."

Steiger shook Candy's hand and reached out to shake Mack's hand. Mack noticed the ring Steiger was wearing. It contained the same design that the others had worn.

"Special Forces, I see," Steiger said shaking Mack's hand.

"Very observant. You serve in the SF too?"

"No, I just recognized the symbol. The closet I ever got was to learn to skydive. Do you still jump?"

"Static line jumping is no fun. I crave the adrenaline rush of free-falling, pulling my chute at the absolute lowest altitude possible. It's that sensation of cheating death that's the real excitement. What about you? You still skydive?"

"Yep. Nearly every weekend. I have a friend who owns his own plane and he takes a small group of us up. You interested in coming along?"

"The idea does intrigue me," Mack responded, "but I don't have any equipment. I would have to try and rent some."

"That's not a problem. I have an extra parachute, altimeter, and jump suit that you can use. It would be great pleasure to skydive with a former Special Forces guy."

"May not be a bad idea," Mack said nodding his head. "Tomorrow's Saturday, and we don't have anything scheduled yet, do we Candy?"

"I do. I wanted to go shopping and maybe get my hair and nails done. That'll take several hours for sure."

"Sounds like a plan then," Steiger said smiling at Mack. "I'll give you a ride out to the airport tomorrow morning at 9:00 a.m. How's that sound? I like to jump in the morning before the temperature gets too high. The thermals can keep you aloft too long and push you outside of the drop zone."

"Don't have that problem," Mack replied. "Waiting until the absolute minimum to deploy the chute takes the problem of the thermals out of the picture. Besides, flirting on the edge of disaster is what makes a man."

"That's what drives me wild about him. I find men who live dangerously, irresistible," Candy said winking at Steiger.

"You a betting man, Paul?" Steiger asked.

"Never one to turn down a challenge," Mack said staring at Steiger. "What do you have in mind?"

"I'll bet that I can free-fall longer than you and open my chute at a lower altitude. Kind of like a game of skydiving chicken."

"What do I get if I win?" Mack asked.

"Twenty-thousand dollars. If I win, I get a night on the town with Candy," Steiger said winking back at Candy.

"Sounds good to me, but I can't speak for Candy."

"Take that bet, Paul. Imagine what we could do with twenty-thousand dollars. There's no way that you can lose."

"Don't start spending that twenty grand just yet," Steiger said with a cocky look on his face. "That night with you is as good as in the bag, or should I say, as good as in the chute," Steiger said laughing out loud.

"We'll see who turns chicken tomorrow."

"I'll pick you up at 9:00 a.m. sharp. If you change your mind, I'll understand," Steiger replied with a hint of arrogance.

"I'll be there, don't worry," Mack said with the same hint of arrogance.

"That's an interesting ring you're wearing," Mack said.

"It's unique. I'm in kind of a professional society. We all wear this ring," Steiger said twisting the ring around his finger.

"Like the Masons?" Mack asked.

"Yeah, something like that. It's an exclusive club. Can't tell you much more than that."

Steiger quickly finished his drink, excused himself, and left the bar.

The next morning, Steiger pulled in front of Mack's hotel at 9:00 a.m. exactly. He was driving a black convertible with the top down.

"Ready to go?" Steiger said as Mack approached the car.

"More than ready," Mack said as he opened the door and got inside the vehicle.

It was a beautiful day in Las Vegas. The sun was shining brightly and the sky was a brilliant blue without a trace of a cloud. Steiger pulled out of the hotel and proceeded to a small airport outside the city limits where they would board the plane for their skydiving adventure. Steiger was silent on the ride to the airport and Mack didn't engage him in any conversation.

Upon arrival at the airport, Steiger parked his car outside one of the hangars located near the edge of the runway. Mack noticed a small, twin engine Dehavilland Twin Otter aircraft with the pilot performing pre-flight operations. Mack and Steiger got out of the car and walked inside the hangar. On a small table, two sets of parachutes, altimeters, and jumpsuits were lying. Steiger walked over to the table and picked up one of the jumpsuits.

"That set of gear is for you," Steiger said pointing to the other set of gear lying on the small table.

"Thanks," Mack said picking up a black jumpsuit and began putting it on.

Mack completed putting on his jump suit and looked closely at the parachute that he would be using for the day's jump. Mack was familiar with this type of parachute. He had used one very similar in nature during his covert operations. Steiger did not bother conducting a safety check on his parachute. He simply picked it up and strapped it on. He then picked up the altimeter, placed it in front of his harness, and put on his helmet. Mack checked his altimeter and determined that the current elevation was 2,030 feet above sea level. Mack adjusted the altimeter to account for the current elevation and determined that he would need to deploy his parachute at least five hundred feet above the ground, the minimum safe distance to ensure a safe landing. Mack completed putting on his gear and accompanied Steiger to the aircraft. The pilot was already onboard and when they entered the aircraft, Steiger gave a "thumbs up" and the pilot started the engines. Within moments, the plane was airborne and climbing its way up to the drop altitude.

"You can still back out," Steiger yelled over the plane's noise from its engines.

"Not a chance," Mack yelled back.

The plane soon climbed to the jump altitude and was orbiting the drop zone in a large, racetrack pattern. Steiger stood up and motioned for Mack to do the same. Steiger stood in the doorway of the aircraft waiting for the green jump light to illuminate. Mack tapped Steiger on the shoulder indicating that he was ready. Steiger stepped through the doorway and into the sky. Mack followed.

Steiger initially flipped upside down, but soon righted himself. Mack stabilized himself and linked up with Steiger, facing each other as they raced toward the ground at 120 miles per hour. Mack and Steiger continued to fall to Earth at an extreme rate. Mack then put himself into a steep dive, increasing his speed to nearly 200 miles per hour. Steiger, not to be outdone by Mack, also put himself into a steep dive and not only caught up to Mack, but continued past him at a very high velocity. Mack quickly slowed his descent by adjusting his body out of the dive and into a position which created more air resistance. Mack looked at his altimeter and realized that he was quickly approaching the safe limit to deploy his parachute. Mack watched intently as Steiger continued to fall in a dive without slowing his descent.

Mack's chute opened and caught the wind. The opening of the chute yanked hard against his harness and slowed his descent with just seconds to spare.

He hit the ground hard. The impact sent a large shock through his body. He was surprised that he remembered how to perform a parachute landing fall, something that he learned to master during his several hundred jumps in combat. Even using this technique, the impact sent excruciating pain through his body. Mack laid on the ground trying to determine if he was injured. He laid still for a few moments, slowly moving his legs. Both legs felt fine, so he started to rise to his feet. His back had taken a significant impact.

He would be sore for a few weeks to come. Mack took off his helmet and noticed that it was scarred from his contact with the ground.

Mack looked around for Steiger. He was nowhere in sight. As he was looking around, a 4x4 truck was approaching him. Mack stood still as the vehicle drove up to him.

"You all right? You took one horrendous hit. We saw you falling and were waiting for you to deploy your chute. We didn't think you were going to get it open. Was there a problem?"

"No, just fixated on the ground and lost all sense of direction and presence. Luckily, I came to my senses in time to deploy my chute," Mack said dishonestly.

"Did you see the other guy's chute open?"

"No, I was concentrating on my own free-fall. No time to see what someone else is doing."

"We didn't either. Looks like he hit the ground in a full dive. I don't think he survived the jump. You guys friends?"

"No, just met him yesterday. He invited me to go skydiving. He let me borrow this equipment."

"Okay, wait here. Another vehicle will come along in fifteen minutes or so. They will take you back to the airport. We were sent out here to pick up two skydivers."

"Can't I just go with you?"

"It would not be a good idea. We need to locate the other skydiver and the scene may be rather gruesome. We saw the whole thing so you won't need to hang around. We'll tell the authorities what we witnessed. Glad you're okay."

"Thanks," said Mack. "I'm shaken up enough without seeing something like that."

While Mack waited for the second vehicle, he took off his

jump suit, stuffed the parachute back inside the pack, and took his helmet and clipped it to the parachute harness. When the second vehicle arrived, Mack threw his gear in the bed of the pickup truck and rode across the desert drop zone. At the airport, Mack dropped his gear on the small table and walked out of the hangar. A police helicopter was crossing the airport on its way to the drop zone. Mack walked out to the street and hitched a ride back into town, walking the last several blocks to his hotel.

Mack returned to his hotel room and was still limping a bit from the sudden impact with the ground. Candy rushed to meet him.

"Paul, you all right? You look hurt. What happened?"

"I'm okay. No broken bones or anything. I just hit the ground a bit hard today during the jump. I'll be sore for a few days, but other than that, no problem," Mack said wincing from the pain.

"What about…"

"Steiger?"

"Is he okay?"

"I don't know. I didn't see his chute open."

"Oh my god…you could have been killed."

"Accidents happen. That's the risk you take when you jump out of a perfectly good airplane."

"Promise me you won't take any more chances." The tears in Candy's eyes began to swell.

"I promise," Mack said.

Mack picked up his cell phone and opened the surveillance program. This time, there was one in each bedroom, one in the living room and one in the bathroom. His mission was becoming more complicated with the introduction of Candy.

"C'mon, I could use a drink," Mack said putting his arm

around Candy.

She grabbed her small purse, slipped on a pair of sandals and followed Mack out of the room. The room was no longer safe to talk freely. Mack and Candy took the elevator back down to the hotel lobby and left the hotel by the front entrance. Mack opened one of the waiting taxi cab doors and allowed Candy to enter. He jumped in the taxi next to her and closed the door.

"Where to?" asked the taxi driver.

"A nice quiet bar. Know any?" Mack asked.

"I know just the place. A little off the beaten path, but it's a nice place to hang out and have a few drinks. Mostly local folks."

"Sounds perfect," Mack replied.

By now, the Nevada sun had started to heat things up. Mack felt the sun's strong rays burning the bare skin on the back of his neck. Las Vegas was a nice place to visit, but not somewhere he wanted to live. Everything in the city revolved around the casinos. The city never slept. Once outside the main city, the taxi cab drove down the highway for a few miles until reaching a small bar off the side of the road. The taxi turned into the stone parking lot and pulled close to the entrance of the bar. The parking lot was rather full for this time of day.

"Here ya go. I think you'll like it. People are friendly enough. They don't stick their noses into other folks' business."

"Thanks, only one problem. How do we get back into town?"

"Just give me a call and I'll come pick you up," the man said handing Mack his business card.

Mack handed the taxi driver a hundred-dollar bill and said "How about picking us up in two hours?"

"Sure thing!" exclaimed the man. "I'll be back in two hours on the dot."

The bar was dark and rustic. Neon signs decorated the walls and the dark wood paneling gave it a warm, welcome feeling. Mack located a small booth along the one wall and slid into the seat. Candy took the seat opposite of Mack. None of the bar patrons seemed to notice that they even walked in. Everyone seemed to be engaged in their own thoughts. The waitress appeared and Mack ordered two beers. The waitress soon returned with the two beers, each garnished with a lime. Mack took a long swig of his beer while Candy took just several sips. The cold beer made Mack feel better.

On a television behind the bar, a breaking news story about a tragic skydiving incident was taking place. Mack grabbed his beer and walked to the bar.

"What's going on?" Mack asked an elderly gentleman sitting at the bar.

"Someone died in a skydiving accident. Looks like his chute didn't open."

"Must have been an equipment malfunction," Mack said.

"Nope. They said that there was nothing wrong with the chute. Authorities say, that based on eyewitness accounts, he got fixated on the ground. They called it target fixation. That's where the skydiver forgets to pull the ripcord because he is so focused on the landing area."

"That's amazing. How could someone forget to pull his ripcord?"

"More common than you think. I flew fighters in World War II. I had to constantly tell myself to pull out when strafing a target. Almost bought the farm on a few occasions. Some of my friends didn't pull up in time. They got so fixated on the target, their brain didn't realize the danger they were in until it was too late."

"Never heard that before," Mack lied.

"That's the risk when you skydive," the elderly man said. "It's not the fall that kills you, it's the sudden stop."

Mack laughed and the elderly gentleman joined in. Mack walked back over to Candy and downed the last portion of his beer. Candy had already finished her beer, so Mack ordered two more.

"Steiger didn't make it."

"You mean he was killed?"

"Yep. Just saw it on the news. Guy over there said that he was too fixated on the ground. Forgot to pull his chute."

"Oh my god. That is horrible. How could he forget to pull his chute?"

"You get so caught up in what you're doing, you don't realize the danger your in." Mack thought how ironic that sounded. *I had better keep my mind in the game.*

"I have to leave tomorrow, but I have one last night here in Vegas with you."

"Well, we'll have to make it last!" Candy said in a flirting fashion.

Nearly two hours had passed since their arrival at the bar. Mack and Candy managed to drink five beers each during the time. Mack pulled out a fifty-dollar bill and asked the waitress if that would cover it. The waitress gave Mack a huge smile and said "Sure thing, honey."

Mack and Candy walked outside of the bar and were immediately hit with intense heat, like a blast out of an oven door. They found some shade created by the roof overhang. Just a few minutes after the two hours had passed, the taxi pulled into the parking lot.

"Sorry I'm late," the taxi driver said. "Got distracted watching the news story on the skydiver who crashed and burned in the desert."

"Yeah, I just watched it myself," admitted Mack. "Someone told me that it was target fixation."

"Don't know about that," spouted the taxi driver. "I think it was a case of pure stupidity myself."

"That too," Mack said.

The taxi ride back to the hotel seemed to take much longer than the ride to the bar. Finally, the taxi pulled into the front entrance of the hotel and Mack handed the driver another hundred-dollar bill. At first, the driver refused the money, but Mack convinced him to take it. The driver left with a huge smile on his face.

Mack and Candy returned to their room and Mack immediately noticed that he had a missed call on his cell phone. It was Rippy. Mack walked into one of the bedrooms, closed the door and dialed the number. Rippy answered on the third ring.

"It's done," Mack said.

"Well done more like it," Rippy said in his normal, solemn tone. "Your next mission is ready. Room service will deliver the envelope with a bottle of champagne. We'll be in touch. Oh, by the way, if you are going to change hotel accommodations next time, I would appreciate a heads up," Rippy said as he hung up the phone.

"Who was that, Paul?"

"Work. Looks like I'll have to leave Las Vegas tomorrow."

"Oh, so soon? I was beginning to really like this place."

"Sorry, I'll make it up to you at a later time. I ordered some champagne and room service should be bringing it up soon. We can have one last night together."

"Well, I guess," Candy said. "Where are you going?"

"Don't know yet. They said they will let me know. I just know that I need to leave tomorrow."

"Seems strange," Candy said.

"Not strange at all. My employer gets notice that there is a project and he gives me as much notice as possible. I'll know sometime tonight. Makes no difference to me. I go wherever they want. Sometimes, I luck out and get to go to Vegas."

Mack was interrupted by a knock at the door. Mack looked through the peep hole and saw a young man dressed in a tan hotel uniform holding a silver bucket containing a bottle of chilled champagne and a brown envelope. Mack took the items then handed him a twenty-dollar bill.

"Champagne is here."

"I'm going to soak in the hot tub for a while. Can you pour me a glass and bring it in?"

"Right away," Mack said opening the bottle and pulling out two champagne glasses from one of the kitchen cabinets. He poured the champagne into both glasses and took them into the bathroom. Candy had not yet disrobed, so Mack blocked the camera's view with his back while Candy got into the hot tub. He handed Candy one of the two glasses and set the other one down on the edge of the tub. Mack left the bathroom and returned to the living room to open the brown envelope.

CHAPTER TEN

Inside the envelope was the same standard letter that he had grown accustomed to seeing. The letter had the words: *James E. Black—Selected for Termination for Crimes against the United States.* As before, the dossier included several photographs of the target. Mack picked up one of the photographs which showed a gentleman in his mid-sixties with thick black hair, dark brown eyes, and a heavy five-o'clock shadow. The location of the target, Lancaster, Pennsylvania, grabbed Mack's immediate attention. He had grown up in a neighboring county and had driven through Lancaster many times. Lancaster was not far from his home in Harrisburg.

Mack looked at the rest of the contents in the envelope. It contained two airline tickets from Las Vegas to Baltimore-Washington International Airport, commonly referred to a "BWI". Mack looked at the names on the tickets. One was in his name "Paul Brittan", but the other ticket was for Candy. Mack smiled to himself. It must benefit him to have Candy back on the east coast, otherwise he would have left it up to Mack to get her home. Mack read the rest of the instructions. He would pick up his vehicle at BWI in the long-term parking area.

Inside the envelope was a parking stub and instructions on where the vehicle was parked. Mack put the contents back into the envelope and put it in his duffle bag. He would finish packing in the morning and catch the 10:00 a.m. flight to BWI. Mack went back into the bathroom and joined Candy in the warm water.

The next morning, Mack checked out of the hotel and they caught a taxi to the airport. The flight back to BWI was full. Rippy did not provide first-class tickets, but at least he was seated next to Candy. After retrieving their bags at the luggage carousel, Mack found the vehicle and drove Candy back to her hotel in Frederick, Maryland.

"I'll be in touch," Mack said with great sadness. "Take care of yourself. I'll call you soon." Candy gave Mack a big hug, hiding her face in Mack's shoulder.

"Please be careful," Candy whispered into Mack's ear.

"Don't worry. I'll be okay," Mack whispered back

Mack left the room without looking back at Candy. He didn't want the last thing he saw to be Candy's sad face.

Mack left the hotel and started the one hour drive to Harrisburg. When he arrived, he drove past his house instead of pulling into the driveway. He noticed that the screen door was not completely closed. *I know I locked it before I left.* Mack parked a few blocks down and walked to the house.

By now, the sun had set and it was quite dark outside. Mack crept up to the house, staying in the shadows. Wearing a black knit shirt and black cargo pants, he was nearly invisible in the darkness. He made his way up to one of the side windows and peeked inside. The room had been disrupted, the couch had been moved, and the cushions had been thrown on the floor. Fortunately, Mack's large flat-screen television was still there, along with the DVD player and home stereo system on the entertainment center located below the television. The kitchen table was littered with remnants of numerous fast-food meals. Then Mack saw movement. A man exited the small bathroom located off of the kitchen, sat down, and pulled a handgun from his waistband, setting it conspicuously on the kitchen table.

Mack made his way around to the back of the house and looked inside the small bathroom window. No one else was in there, and the door was closed. *Good.* Pulling himself into the bathroom, he waited a moment for his eyes to adjust. Mack made his way across the room and quietly opened the door a crack. The man's back was towards Mack, and he was eating French fries. The kitchen was illuminated by several nightlights. Mack would have the element of surprise on his side. Pushing the door open, he reached the table in three steps and grabbed the handgun before the man realized that he was there.

Mack struck the man on the side of his head rendering him unconscious. The man slumped over the kitchen table. Mack checked the rest of the house quickly, but did not find anyone else inside. The front screen door had been pried open and the main door had damage. Mack made his way back to the kitchen where the man was still slumped over the table. He searched the man for any additional weapons and found a black, titanium lock blade knife in the man's back pocket. Mack bound the man's hands behind his back with flex cuffs. Then he bound the man's feet to the chair.

Mack also located a cell phone in the man's jacket pocket. He looked at the numbers dialed and didn't recognize any of the numbers except they were from a California area code. The numbers received were nearly identical to the numbers dialed. The man had been receiving calls every two hours. According to the call log, it had only been fifteen minutes since the last call.

Mack searched the man more closely this time. Inside the jacket pocket he found two pieces of paper. Mack unfolded them and saw a color portrait of his driver's license photo. *How the heck did they get that?* The second piece of paper contained a photograph of Mack taken by the surveillance cameras during the operation to terminate Osterman. The writing on the paper below the photograph read *"Russian/Serbian/Ukrainian. Extremely dangerous—hold until backup arrives."* Mack laughed to himself. *Russian? Where did they get that from?* Mack then yanked the man upright by his hair.

"Who are you?" Mack said in a Russian accent.

"Screw you," the man said in a New Jersey accent.

Mack grabbed a glass from the kitchen cabinet and filled it with cold water.

"I'll ask you again. Who are you?"

"I'll say it again, Screw You!"

Mack grabbed the man's hair and yanked his head back as far as it would go. He took the glass of water and started pouring the contents down the nose and mouth of the man. The man began to choke and gasp for air.

"Stop. Stop."

"I'll stop when you start talking," Mack said pouring more water into the man's nose.

It was getting harder and harder for the man to breathe. Mack stopped pouring long enough for the man to catch his breath. Mack waited for the man to respond. Hearing nothing, Mack tipped the glass forward again.

"Stop! Stop! I'll tell you what you want to know."

"Who sent you here?"

"Nobody. I came by myself."

"Listen to me. Carefully. You have one chance to tell me what I want to know. Otherwise, I will start with the water again, but this time, I will boil it first."

All the color drained from the man's face.

"J-Johnson."

"I don't know any Johnson. You got to do better than that," Mack said raising the glass again and moving it towards the man.

"I swear to you, his name is Johnson. I don't know his first name. I was given two photographs of you and your address. I was told to wait, no matter how long it took, until you came home. Then I was to hold you until help arrived. That's all I know."

"You know more than that," Mack said as the anger started to grow inside of him. "I need more names."

"Becker … Becker. That is who Johnson said I would have to deal with if I screwed up. He's supposed to be ruthless."

Mack had heard that name before. In the dossier on Osterman, Rippy had stated that Becker was Osterman's enforcer. Now things started to make sense. Becker was attempting to track down the person, or persons, involved in the death of Osterman. Mack had all the information that he needed from this man. If Becker was inclined to think that the Russians were somehow involved, then Mack could continue this ruse and throw Becker completely off the trail.

"I am going to let you live for one reason," Mack said. "You tell Becker that Osterman crossed the Russian mob. If he wants to wind up the same way as Osterman, he had better do what we say."

The man nodded his head. Mack picked up the man's cell phone and dialed the California number. Johnson answered on the second ring.

"You better have good news for me."

"Shut up and listen," Mack said in his Russian accent. "You have made a grave mistake. Tell Becker that I know who he is and that I'll be coming for him." Switching to Russian, Mack said, "And I won't stop until he is dead."

Mack hung up the phone. He needed to leave the house quickly. He didn't know if any others were nearby and didn't want to risk a confrontation at this point. Mack memorized Johnson's cell phone number and threw the phone on the table as he walked out of the house.

Johnson couldn't believe his ears. He didn't speak Russian, so he didn't know the last thing Mack told him. Johnson immediately called his contacts in New York and told them that their man might be dead. Johnson then called Becker.

"Sir, we have a development. There is something that you need to hear."

"What is it?" Becker bellowed into the phone.

"Looks like our New York contacts failed. We got a phone call from the guy, or at least I think it was the guy. He mentioned your name specifically."

"I'll be right there," Becker said as he hung up the phone.

Within moments, Becker was in the compound's security office. Johnson already had the recording cued up and ready to go. Becker listened carefully to the message and asked Johnson to replay it several times.

"Russians," Becker said. "I want to know exactly what he said at the end of the conversation. Find someone who speaks Russian and get that translated."

"Already on it, Boss. One of the girls is Russian. I sent for her right after I called you. She should be here any minute."

Within a minute, two guards arrived with Ivanka in tow.

"Ivanka, I want you to listen to something. You speak Russian right?" Becker asked.

"Born and raised in Russia."

Johnson cued up the recording again, this time for Ivanka to listen. She listened carefully to the recording and asked to hear it again to make sure of what she heard.

He said, "And I won't stop until he is dead."

Becker didn't even flinch. "So, this guy's Russian?"

"Absolutely," Ivanka said. "I don't know what part of Russia; there are so many dialects, but there is no doubt, the voice on that tape is Russian."

"Thanks. That's all I needed," Becker said as he motioned for Johnson to escort the girl out. Becker left the security office and went to his private office to telephone the regional bosses.

"We have new information."

"Well, don't make me friggin' ask for it," the boss said with impatience.

"Looks like it's the Russians. He captured one of our guys who was sitting inside his home waiting for him. Our guy must have talked. The Russian called and left a message for me."

"What kind of message?"

"He told me that Osterman got hit because he crossed the mob. He told me that he was coming to kill me," Becker said half laughing.

"We don't need a war with the Russians," the boss said. "Osterman is dead. You're in charge now. You start a war with the Russians, and I'll deal with you personally. Catch my drift?"

"Got the message," Becker said as the boss hung up the phone.

Becker had got what he wanted. He was now the boss. One still bothered him. If this guy was just a member of the Russian mob, then why did this guy's picture draw major attention at the CIA and Pentagon? Becker was still suspicious that the U.S. government was involved. Unless he had solid evidence, he would not bring up the subject again with the regional bosses. He would deal with this Russian in the event that he tried to kill him.

CHAPTER ELEVEN

LANCASTER, PENNSYLVANIA
0300 hours

Mack arrived in the middle of the night. Rippy arranged a hotel near Manheim, a small town near the city of Lancaster. Mack checked into his room and pulled out the dossier to study the target and plan his mission. James E. Black, or "JEB" as people called him, owned a large farm in Lancaster County. The dossier indicated that Jeb was operating a major methamphetamine laboratory, and the farm was merely a front. Mack had some knowledge of the manufacturing of methamphetamine. He knew that a chemical used by farmers called anhydrous ammonia was used in the manufacturing process. Farmers and agricultural facilities across the country had reported thefts of this chemical by manufacturers of this drug. Black's ownership of a large farm would allow him to obtain this chemical without any suspicion. Manufacturing the drug on a farm in a mostly rural county would draw even less suspicion. If done properly, Black could have a professional quality laboratory set up on the farm, and none would be the wiser.

Mack would need to conduct surveillance to determine the best plan of action. If possible, Mack would make Black's demise appear like an accident. *Perhaps a meth lab explosion?* The problem with an explosion is that it may cause the chemicals to spread out over a large area. The last thing Mack wanted was for others to be injured. He would have to find a way to eliminate Black without endangering innocent people.

Mack awoke early the next morning. His thoughts turned to Candy. He hoped that she was fine. He wished that she were with him, but he knew that it was better that she was not involved in this operation. He could fully concentrate on the task at hand and know that she would be safe, at least for now.

Mack left his hotel and headed towards the Black farm. Rippy had provided a couple of satellite images. The farm appeared to be like any other. A long lane led from the main road to the buildings, which included a farm house, a large barn, and two silos. Located near the barn was another building, rectangular in shape, with several large storage tanks nearby that Mack suspected contained the anhydrous ammonia. This rectangular building probably contained the laboratory where the drug was being manufactured. He would conduct surveillance from a distance during the daytime and wait for the cover of darkness to go on-site for a closer look.

Mack found a small restaurant and pulled in to get some breakfast. As he entered the building he immediately saw women wearing long dresses with their hair pulled up and covered with a white lace head covering. Mack immediately recognized these women as Mennonites. Mack ordered breakfast and was pleased with the portion size that he received. The food was made from scratch and reminded him of the meals that he had as a child. His mother would make him waffles every Sunday morning and then always tease him about the large amount of syrup he dumped on top of them. Mack finished his breakfast, smiling to himself that he recalled another memory of his mother.

The young Mennonite waitress gave him a big smile when Mack told her that he didn't need any change. Mack thought how much better the country would be if everyone had the morals and ethics of the Mennonites. If that was the case, the country wouldn't need his services. Mack laughed to himself. *If only they knew that they just served breakfast to an assassin.*

Mack jumped in his truck and entered the address in his GPS. He followed the directions to the area near the farm and started looking for a place to conduct surveillance. He found a small road leading north away from the farm. Mack drove up the road and found that it led to a small church and cemetery. He pulled into the cemetery and turned his vehicle so that the passenger-side window faced south towards the farm. Less than half a mile away, Mack had a clear view of the laboratory. This would be an excellent place to conduct surveillance without raising suspicions. If anyone came up the road, Mack would have sufficient time to stash his equipment.

Mack pulled out a high-definition video camera from his backpack, then placed it on top of the tripod. Mack turned the camera on and zoomed in on the building. The 600x zoom lens brought the image into clear view on the LCD screen. Mack focused in on what appeared to be the only entrance door. About an hour later, a large man, dressed in blue overhauls and a plaid shirt, walked towards the laboratory from the farm house. It was Black. Mack pushed the record button and followed him with the camera.

Black opened the door to the laboratory and stepped inside. He emerged a few moments later and stood outside making a phone call. Mack zoomed in on Black's hand. There it was, a large gold ring on Black's left hand, something that a real farmer would never wear. Black finished his call and stepped back inside.

Thirty minutes later, a cargo van drove down the lane to the farm house and stopped in front of the laboratory. The driver entered the building returning a few moments later carrying a large cardboard box. Black was following close behind carrying an identical box. They shook hands and the man gave Black a duffle bag, which Black unzipped to look inside. Apparently pleased by what he saw, Black shook the man's hand again. As the man drove away, Black took the duffle bag into the laboratory. A few minutes later, Black came out and walked towards the farmhouse, got into an old, blue pickup, and drove down the lane.

Mack turned off the video camera and placed it on the passenger floorboard. He pulled out of the cemetery and down towards the farm. Black reached the main road first and turned west. Mack also turned west and followed him at a safe distance, weaving their way between dozens and dozens of farms. They passed numerous Amish folks driving their horse and buggies. Mack wondered how that life style still continued to exist despite the entire world moving forward in time and technology. Mack did notice that he never saw on overweight Amish man. Hard work had kept these men in great physical shape, something that today's society could take a lesson from.

Black pulled into the restaurant where Mack had eaten breakfast several hours earlier. Black got out of his truck and walked inside. Mack pulled into the parking lot and parked next to Black's truck. Mack followed him into the restaurant and noticed the he had already taken a seat at the counter. Following Black's lead, Mack took a seat at the counter, just two stools down and to the left of Black.

"Jeb, how's it going?" the waitress asked.

"Not bad. What's the special today?"

"Chicken potpie."

"I'll have that."

"Sounds good," Mack said. "I'll have one too."

"You won't be disappointed," Black said.

Mack couldn't help but notice Black's ring. Its shape was slightly different from the five previous ones he had seen, but the insignia was identical. His hands were not calloused, his boots were not laden with mud, and his overalls were too clean for a farmer. Black looked like the chemist he was, dressed up like a farmer for Halloween.

Black had spent the majority of his life as a chemist. He was once world renowned for his research in molecular chemistry, an occupation that brought much more prestige than money. Black had done some top secret work for the government to develop a chemical that could be sprayed on enemy forces which would destroy their will to fight. This information was accidentally leaked to a news reporter and Black's work on the program was halted. The government accused Black as the source of the leak, discontinued his research, and his employment as a result. He held great resentment towards the government now. Black had made significant progress in developing the chemical. He surmised that the government didn't want to pay him for his discovery, so they concocted a story to get rid of him. It was then that he had a "chance meeting" with a stranger.

This stranger convinced Black the government had indeed stolen his work. He also convinced Black that his knowledge would be much more useful, and profitable, by joining the organization. This secret society would provide Black with all that he desired. Black was enticed to join by the ability to obtain whatever he wanted, whenever he wanted it. All he had to do in return was to use his knowledge as a chemist to benefit the organization.

He was given the task of manufacturing methamphetamine.

This drug was inexpensive to produce, but was extremely profitable. The street value of this drug per once was far more valuable than any precious metal or gems. He was provided with the farm where he oversaw the construction of the laboratory. In order to not raise suspicion, Black used the laboratory to do chemical analysis of soil. Many of the local farmers provided Black with soil samples from their fields and Black would provide a detailed analysis with the proper mix of chemicals needed to maximize crop growth. It was Black, through the use of this laboratory, who conducted chemical analysis of the explosive used to terminate Osterman.

Black had been operating the laboratory for several years. His production of methamphetamine for the organization netted millions of dollars. As a member, he was entitled to one-twelfth of all the profits. Each member had access to draw money for the organizational account which now totaled over two billion dollars. Any member requesting a withdrawal of more than five hundred thousand dollars however, required the approval of the majority of all members. In the event of the death of one of its members, their share in the account was forfeited. The last surviving member would "inherit" the full amount.

There was no leaving the organization. The only way out was death. Meetings were only held once a year. The meetings took place in a predetermined location where each member sat around a large, circular table. Each member would wear special robes with large hoods which hid their faces. Names were never used, so each member did not know the other's names or appearance. The leader would be the only one who spoke at the meetings. He would provide items to be voted on and would read each proposal to the members. Members voted approval of the proposal by tapping their ring on the table, each taking their turn to vote as they went around the table. If a member did not agree with the proposal, he would not tap his ring when it was his turn to vote.

Black had only been to six annual meetings. He had asked for money on the first two occasions and was given approval. However, each subsequent time that he asked for money, he was turned down. Black had been making tens of millions of dollars for the organization and although he was entitled to one-twelfth share, getting his hands on it once it went into the account was nearly impossible.

Black then started to take his cut from the money he received from the sale of methamphetamine. Because the cost to manufacture was so low, Black would cook up a couple of extra batches and sell them on the side. He had arranged a deal with his customers that he would add additional drugs to the order at a discounted price and they would pay for them separately. The organization expected him to bring in a certain amount of money each month. He never shorted the organization's share for fear of retribution, but he made his own profit outside their knowledge, or at least he thought.

Black had no clue that the person sitting two stools down was an assassin hired to terminate him. He also had no knowledge that five members of the organization had already been eliminated. He did not know any of their names, nor had he seen their faces. As far as Black knew, there were eleven other members operating throughout the world, each contributing to the organizational account.

If Black wanted a woman, all he had to do was to call the number provided and he would receive a phone call where to meet her. If he needed money for the operation of the laboratory, he called the same number and a package would arrive the next day filled with cash. He made sure that this money was spent on laboratory expenses. Black had once asked for an assistant to help him run the lab to increase the amount of drugs being manufactured, but was denied. Black was directed to run the lab by himself. The more people who knew about the lab and its operation increased the chances of its discovery by the authorities.

Mack finished his chicken potpie and the waitress took his plate. "That hit the spot," Mack said.

"I told you that you wouldn't be disappointed," Black said.

"Glad I took your advice," Mack said pulling out cash to pay his bill. As before, Mack left a generous tip which pleased the waitress.

"Catch you around sometime," Mack said to Black as he rose from his stool.

"Highly likely if you come here again to eat. I eat lunch and dinner here almost every day, except Sunday because they're closed."

"I'll have to keep that in mind."

Mack left the restaurant and jumped in his truck. He now knew where Black would be on certain days and certain times. Mack figured the best time to strike would be Sunday since the restaurant would be closed. He also wouldn't have to worry about any farmers bringing soil samples to the laboratory because the local farmers didn't conduct business on Sunday. Mack drove back to the hotel and began to develop his action plan.

Mack sat in his room and pulled out the dossier on Black. The medical information in the file indicated that Black had a weak heart and took nitroglycerin for chest pains. Perhaps Mack could facilitate the onset of a heart attack. This option would raise the least suspicion. He would pursue this first and resort to more traditional methods if necessary. He could also make it look like a major drug deal gone bad. The authorities would have no problem believing this scenario once they uncovered the large methamphetamine lab. However, they would be looking for the person, or persons, involved in the murder.

Mack laid down for a few hours of sleep. Today was Saturday, so tonight would be a perfect time to strike. If Black was telling Mack the truth, he would be eating dinner at the Farmer's Daughter restaurant this evening. Mack fell asleep with Candy on his mind. After tonight, his mission would be half completed. He considered telling Rippy that he had done enough, but the likelihood of Rippy letting Mack, or Candy for that matter, just walk away was zero. Besides, Rippy had to be involved somehow. Mack decided that he would question Black about the organization before his demise. Rippy would have no idea what Mack learned. That would be his ace in the hole.

When Mack awoke it was still daylight. He dressed in his usual black pants, boots, and jacket. He placed a small .22 caliber pistol in his pocket, something that he had a permit for to carry in Pennsylvania. An assassin who has a concealed weapons permit. *How funny was that?* Mack thought. Mack left the hotel and drove back out to the cemetery that overlooked Black's farm. Mack had stopped at a small gas station and bought some tea and beef jerky. He also bought some flowers at the store as deception if anyone was at the cemetery while he was there. He was glad that he did. When he arrived at the cemetery, there were several cars in the small church parking lot. He could hear organ music coming from inside the church. Mack parked his vehicle and walked into the cemetery with the flowers. He had a clear view of the farm including Black's old blue pickup truck.

The sun was starting to set, casting long shadows across the ground. The setting sun, the stillness of the air, and the organ music made for a very tranquil setting. Mack spotted a small grave marker beside a larger headstone. He walked over to the small marker and learned that it was a child that was buried there. His heart almost broke. He couldn't imagine the parent's pain when they lost this child. Mack knelt down next to the grave and laid the flowers down. He said a little prayer to himself asking that comfort be given to all those who loved this child.

Mack watched the farm and soon saw Black leaving in his old blue truck. Mack knew where he was headed, no need to follow. Mack got back into his truck and drove out of the cemetery. He would drive down past the restaurant just to ensure Black was there. He would then drive out to the farm and hide his truck and wait for Black to return. As predicted, Mack saw the truck in the parking lot as he drove past. It was almost dark. By the time he drove the few miles to the farm, it would be completely dark. He turned down the long lane and switched off his headlights. He didn't want anyone seeing him coming or going. Pulling around the back side of the large barn, he hid his vehicle from view.

Mack made his way up to the old farm house and put on a pair of black gloves. He approached the same door that he saw Black enter and exit several times. Mack found the door unlocked and pushed it open. Mack quickly scanned the room for any indication of an alarm system. He didn't see any sensors on the wall or an alarm keypad by the door. The small farm house living room was dimly lit by several nightlights. It was warm with the familiar smell of a fireplace. The kitchen was old and outdated. It lacked the modern conveniences such as a dishwasher or large refrigerator.

An old refrigerator sat in the corner of the kitchen and rattled slightly. There was a small wooden table against one of the walls which was laden with bread, cheese, pretzels and other snacks.

The house had a musty smell about it, as if the windows had not been opened for many years. Mack walked into the small living room and saw a large fireplace. It appeared to have been updated recently with fresh stonework and a large cherry mantel. On either side of the fireplace were large bookcases filled with books on chemistry. In front of the fireplace were two brown leather chairs with matching ottomans. In between the two chairs was a cherry table with a reading lamp. Also on the table was a crystal decanter filled with cognac and two glass brandy snifters. Mack had to hand it to Black, this living room was very inviting. Had situations been different, Mack would have really enjoyed sitting in one of the chairs in front of a warm fire, sipping cognac and engaging in intelligent conversation. Mack took a seat in one of the chairs and waited for Black to return.

Mack could see the farm's lane from his seat near the fireplace. He watched as Black's vehicle entered the lane and drove towards the farm house. Black parked his vehicle next to the house and walked into the kitchen. After turning on a small light, he put his keys on the table and took off his jacket. He then walked into to living room and picked up some firewood and started to stack it in the fireplace.

"No need for a fire," Mack said snapping on the reading lamp.

Black spun around quickly and saw Mack sitting in the chair holding a pistol. "Who are you? What do you want? Leave or I'll call the police," Black said very nervously.

"Go ahead, call the police. I'm sure they'll be real interested in the large meth lab you are running out there. Life in prison for sure."

"What do you want? Why are you here?" Black asked again.

"You know why I am here," Mack said.

"You got your money. I met my monthly goals to the organization. I tried to increase production for greater profit, but you refused. So, I kept the extra profits that you didn't want."

"Tell me what you know about the organization," Mack said to Black motioning for him to sit in the chair next to him. "Tell me everything you know or else."

Black proceeded to tell Mack what he knew about the organization. He told Mack how he was recruited after the government terminated his research and the annual meetings that followed. Mack was particularly interested in the person that recruited him.

"What did the guy look like that recruited you?"

Black described in great deal a person who could be Rippy. Mack asked if he knew the name of the person that recruited him, but Black said that names were never used. He was to call this person "Mr. Smith". Black knew that this was not his real name. One piece of information that Black did provide to Mack was that the voice who spoke at the annual meetings was very close to Mr. Smith's. He wasn't one hundred percent sure, but he was nearly certain. Black said it made sense that Mr. Smith was the leader of the organization.

"You've been sent here to kill me?"

"What do you think?" Mack replied.

"Doesn't matter," Black said looking at the fireplace. "Can I have one last request?"

"Depends on what it is," said Mack.

"Let me build a fire and have a final drink of cognac."

"As long as you don't try anything funny," Mack said pointing the gun at Black.

"I give you a dead man's word. You just showed up a day early that's all."

"Day early, what are you talking about?"

"I've been diagnosed with a very rare disease. Unfortunately, it is terminal. There is no hope. My body will deteriorate slowly at first, and then more rapidly. The deterioration process had begun some time ago and it is starting to increase. I decided at the time of my diagnosis that once the deterioration started, I would get my affairs in order and go out on my terms." Black said staring off into space.

"Doesn't explain a day early," Mack said.

"I was planning on killing myself tomorrow. I can prove it," Black said starting to rise from his chair.

"Sit down," Mack said sternly.

"I was going to show you a document that I wrote, that's all. It is not a trick."

"Fine, get your document. If this is a trick, you will regret it," Mack said pointing the gun at Black.

Black rose from his chair and grabbed two white envelopes from the bookshelf closest to him and handed them to Mack.

"Go ahead and read them. They are dated for tomorrow."

Mack opened the first envelope which was not sealed. Inside the envelope was Black's last will and testament. Mack quickly scanned the document. All the possessions were to be sold and the proceeds given to charity. Mack folded the will and placed it back inside the envelope and handed it back to Black.

"Look at the second letter," Black said pointing at the other envelope Mack had in his hand.

Mack opened the unsealed envelope and reads its contents. The letter was a suicide note. It was signed and dated with tomorrow's date. In the note, Black apologized for the terrible things that he had done against society. The note did not include any mention of the organization. Mack folded the note, placed it back in its envelope, and handed it back to Black.

"Now you understand?" Black asked.

"I think so," Mack said.

"I want to die on my terms," Black said sealing both envelopes. "I know the end result would be the same if you were to kill me, but I want the decision to be mine."

"How do you know that I am here to kill you?"

"I don't. I just assumed. If you are, then there isn't anything that I can do about it. If you aren't, then I can proceed with my plans."

"Then the decision to live or die will be in your hands, Jeb," Mack said putting the gun back into his pocket. "I don't kill the sick or the helpless."

"Thank you. My choice has already been made. There is nothing that you, or anyone else for that matter, can do to change my mind."

"Go ahead. Build your fire in the fireplace," Mack said as he arose out of his chair. "If you choose life, you need to disappear where nobody can find you. I mean nobody, especially the organization. Who do you think sent me here?"

"I wish we had met under different circumstances," Black said. "I wish we had met before I joined the organization."

"Me too."

Mack walked to his truck and drove down the lane to the main road. Mack knew what Black was about to do. It was clear that

Black regretted turning his back on his government and leading a life of crime. Now that Mack was certain that Rippy was the leader, he knew the terminations were not ordered by the U.S. Government. Mack drove back to the hotel, but it took him a long time to fall asleep.

CHAPTER TWELVE

ALBUQUERQUE, NEW MEXICO
1630 hours

After receiving his next mission, Mack arrived in Albuquerque, New Mexico late in the afternoon. The flight had been overbooked and Mack gave up his seat to a lady traveling with a small child. Unfortunately, his new seat was in the middle of the aircraft between two very obese women. The women chatted continuously to each other during the whole flight. Mack offered to exchange seats so the women could sit together, but they refused, saying that they were comfortable where they were. Mack sure wasn't. He was never happier to get off an airplane in his life.

Albuquerque was the largest city in New Mexico with a population of more than half a million people and was one of the fastest growing cities in the country. Mack noticed on the flight in that it spread out over a vast distance with few high-rise buildings. Albuquerque did not need to build upwards like most cities; there was plenty of land to expand outwards. The Sandia Mountains, which ran along the eastern side of the city, seemed to rise out of the ground, stretching to reach the desert sun. The mountains were named for the Spanish word for "watermelon" because of their red color. The late afternoon sun turned the mountains a dark reddish color. In this desert community, nature put on a fabulous art display each evening. The lower the sun set into the horizon, the more grandly the mountains appeared. Several white, puffy clouds hung lazily across the top, casting their shadows on the valley below. There was a peace and tranquility about this place that pleased Mack. This was a place where he could live.

Mack's perspiration was drying as soon as it reached the surface of his skin. The low humidity seemed to draw all the moisture out of his body and the elevation affected his breathing. During his training, Mack was taught to recognize even the slightest change in his body's condition. He had learned to hold his breath for over five minutes, recognizing his body's reaction to the lack of oxygen and learning how to take control over his body's need to survive.

The city was more than five-thousand feet above sea level, the air thinner and containing less oxygen. He adjusted his breathing, taking fuller and deeper breaths to account for the lower concentrations of oxygen in the air. It would take several weeks for a normal person to become fully acclimatized to this change in elevation. Mack didn't need the several weeks it would require, he acclimatized his body in a matter of hours. Mack's adjusted breathing rhythm was already starting to become part of his subconscious. He could feel the increased levels of oxygen flowing through his body. One of the things that Mack understood, only too well, is that each mission was highly unpredictable. He was preparing himself in case the mission involved great physical exertion.

Mack picked up his vehicle and left the airport. The sun had now set and the city was aglow with the thousands of street lights. Mack drove to the hotel which was on the outskirts of the city. As he pulled into the hotel, he couldn't believe that he was at the correct address. This was the worst accommodations that Rippy had provided thus far. The hotel was "L" shaped with rows of rooms only on two floors. The entrance to all the rooms was from the outside. All of the room's doors were dented or smashed. The hotel was rundown and in need of heavy maintenance. The paint was peeling from the outside walls and trash was littering the parking lot. Mack parked his vehicle directly in front of his room, his headlights shining into the room's only window. Mack grabbed his duffle bag out of his vehicle.

Several young men were drinking beer on the second level above him. As Mack got near his room, one of the young men threw a beer bottle down towards Mack. The bottle crashed against the wall, spraying glass in numerous directions. Mack didn't flinch. He heard the men laughing as he opened the room with a silver key attached to a large keychain.

The hotel had not been updated in a long time. The room was musty and damp. The old air conditioner below the room's window spewed dust and a moldy odor into the air. Mack switched off the air conditioner and it rattled to a stop. He would rather be uncomfortable than to sleep with that horrible machine running all night. He noticed a large deadbolt lock on the inside of the door. The door jamb had been replaced multiple times. He would leave the door open tonight, hoping that someone tried to enter his room. He hoped, even more, that it would be the scumbag that threw the beer bottle. One thing was sure, whoever entered Mack's room was in for one heck of a surprise.

Mack tossed his duffle bag on one of two chairs next to the bed. The chairs were stained and torn. This hotel looked like it was rented by the hour. Mack couldn't believe that a national hotel chain would own such a nasty place. The bedspread was old and he didn't want to touch it, much less sleep on it. He could only imagine who had been in that bed. Mack considered changing hotels, but decided to wait. So far, Rippy provided him accommodations with some type of connection to the mission.

Mack couldn't imagine what connection this hotel had to the mission, but he would stay for now. Besides, he needed to stay at the hotel at least one night to have a little "fun" with whomever entered his room in the middle of the night.

Mack pulled out the dossier on Quinn and began to study his target. Preparation was the key to success. He studied all the dossiers extremely carefully, committing all the information to memory. Each detail, no matter how small, could provide the advantage he needed in a given situation.

Quinn was an attorney that represented organized crime figures. He would represent any client, no matter how horrendous the crime. He was responsible for the defense of Philip Osterman during Osterman's multiple encounters with the criminal justice system. It was said that he had sold his soul to the devil for doing whatever it took to get his clients acquitted.

Quinn had drawn national media attention over the years by his flamboyant actions in the courtroom. The news media loved airing stories on him. Despite his connections with the mob, Quinn had a celebrity-like status with the media. If Quinn couldn't try his case in the courtroom, he would try it in the news media. He had a flare for the dramatics and was best known for his emotional outbursts during a trial that, on occasion, got him held in contempt of court. He had been accused of being involved in jury tampering through bribery and intimidation. However, it was never more than speculation as the government never had solid evidence to bring formal charges against him. It wasn't as if the government never tried. Jurors, who were initially willing to provide evidence against Quinn, later recanted their stories for fear of retribution by Quinn's clients.

From the photographs of Quinn, he appeared to be in his late fifties or early sixties. He had bright blue eyes, blonde hair which was now mostly grey, and a large mustache. Quinn's face showed years of exposure to the sun. His skin was thick, almost leather-like. He was tall, more than six feet, and very thin.

Quinn's flamboyant courtroom actions were only outdone by his dress and attire. He wanted it to appear as though he was an old-west gunslinger taking on all challengers. He was known to spend hours drawing his pistol from the holster as if practicing for a gunfight in the middle of an old-west town. Quinn often dressed in old western apparel and openly carried a cowboy style six-shooter when he was out in public. He once thwarted a robbery attempt by drawing his six-shooter and pistol whipping the would-be robbers. Quinn had been fortunate not to have killed the robbers. He was nearly criminally charged himself for turning aggressor once the situation had been defused. The dossier also stated that Quinn carried a knife and derringer pistol in his boots. Mack paid close attention to this particular fact.

Quinn spent most of his time in his law office. He didn't have a law partner or any associates. He did have a legal secretary, but she left the office every day at 5 p.m. Quinn was known to work late into the night writing his legal briefs and preparing for trial. His work ethic was second to none. Prosecutors knew that they had better be fully prepared because Quinn was always ready for trial. Once he got involved in a case, he was like a pit-bull, not relinquishing his grip.

He was currently involved in a trial where members of organized crime were charged with homicide. The murders were particularly heinous. An entire family had been murdered when the father refused to cooperate with the mob. The father, devastated by the loss of his entire family, turned government witness. Quinn had a huge uphill battle to obtain acquittals for his clients. He had attempted to bribe or intimidate the jury. However, this time his efforts were thwarted by the government.

In the past, Quinn would learn the names and addresses of the jurors. He would then single out a few jurors that he considered weak and either bribe or intimidate them to render a not guilty verdict. All he needed was one juror to obtain a deadlocked vote. The prosecution has to get all twelve guilty votes in order to convict. Although he was allowed to ask potential jurors questions during jury selection, he was not provided their names. Quinn vehemently objected to the judge, but despite all the courtroom antics and drama, he was overruled. The judge ruled that the names of the jurors did not have any impact on whether they could be fair and impartial. As an additional level of protection, the jurors were sequestered and under heavy security. There was no way that Quinn would be able to influence or intimidate this jury. Changing tactics, Quinn had attempted to stall the trial, giving him more time to influence the jury. The judge was wise to Quinn's antics and kept the trial moving forward.

Quinn was not having any luck. He had considered intentionally forcing a mistrial requiring the start of a new trial, but the judge warned him that if he did, he would be spending more time in jail than his clients. He was out of options. The government had a star witness whose family had been slaughtered. The trial was not going well for Quinn or his clients. He had been paid a very large sum of money and was handed a note in court one day which informed him of dire consequences if his clients were convicted.

Quinn was visibly shaken by the note. He asked for a recess to regain his composure. The judge was reluctant to grant the recess, but did so after noticing that Quinn's demeanor had changed dramatically. Gone was his cocky attitude and flare for the dramatics. The color had disappeared from his face and Quinn had a difficult time concentrating on the task at hand. The judge asked what the contents of the notes contained, but Quinn refused. He would only say it was a matter of life or death.

Several years ago, Quinn was recruited, a perfect choice as the attorney for the organization. His connections to organized crime ensured his secrecy about the organization and its operation. He was kept in line by mounds of incriminating evidence that the authorities could use to put Quinn away for life. The organization needed an attorney to keep one step ahead of the law. Quinn helped set up numerous off-shore accounts and shadow companies to hide the hundreds of millions of dollars brought into the organization. He had vast experience in hiding money for organized crime syndicates. He used his skills to the maximum benefit. Only three men knew where this money was located. The Leader, Quinn, and Steiger. The organization had its tentacles in both legitimate and non-legitimate enterprises throughout the globe. The organization had its assets diversified in large corporations, stocks, bonds, and large amounts of gold and precious metal. Quinn knew much more about the operation than any other member except the Leader. Quinn was both an asset and a liability.

Quinn was aware, without anyone's knowledge, that Osterman had been a member of the organization. Quinn knew both Osterman's appearance and voice. Although all of the members' appearances were covered by hoods, and that no-one ever spoke, Quinn ran into Osterman each time the organization had its annual meets. It wasn't hard for Quinn to put the pieces together to link Osterman to the "Ring of Twelve". Both wore a ring with the same insignia inscribed on it.

Quinn also knew that Osterman had been killed and that the blame was being placed on the Russian mob. Quinn was concerned that his life was in danger. He was paranoid of the Russian mob. He facilitated the negotiations between the mob and Osterman which ended poorly. He was also a potential target by the organized crime syndicate whose members were on trial. The note handed to him in trial that day confirmed Quinn's suspicion. Quinn knew that an attempt on his life would be coming. He didn't know if it would be the Russian mob or the organized crime syndicate. It didn't matter, Quinn would have to deal with each threat as it appeared. He was running scared and knew that if the trial was likely to result in convictions, the syndicate would try to terminate him thereby allowing the trial to start all over again. The trial could not continue without the lead defense attorney.

Mack finished reading the dossier and destroyed the contents in the hotel's business center shredder. He walked out of his room and threw his duffle bag in his vehicle. The young men were still drinking beer on the second floor and taunted Mack as he got into his vehicle. He prayed that they would still be there when he returned.

He left the hotel and drove to the address of Quinn's law office. The law office was in a downtown location with a sign above the entrance that read *"Thomas G. Quinn, Attorney-at-Law."* The office was sandwiched between two larger office buildings, separated on each side by a small alley that was only wide enough for a person to walk through.

Mack parked his vehicle and walked down the dark, narrow alley toward a light shining through a window on the side of the law office. Mack walked up to the window and looked into the room through the partially opened wooden blinds. The blinds shielded the view of the outside from within, but were open enough to view the room from the outside. The area just inside the window appeared to be a small conference room with a wooden table in the center. The conference table was surrounded by six leather chairs with one high back chair at the head of the table. Lining the conference room were dark colored bookcases filled with law books and materials. Some of the law books were open and lying on the conference table.

Across the conference room, Mack saw a man fitting Quinn's description sitting at desk working on a computer. Mack noticed the large, gold ring the man was wearing on his left hand. He wasn't close enough to see the insignia on the ring, but he knew it contained the symbol of the "Ring of Twelve". There was no doubt; this man was Thomas G. Quinn. He was dressed in old western style attire and Mack noticed a silver colored six-shooter sitting on the desk next to Quinn's laptop. Quinn picked up the pistol and twirled it, each time stopping with the hammer cocked and in the firing position. It was clear that he had years of practice performing this trick. Mack scanned the walls of the conference room looking for any indication of an alarm system. He noticed an alarm sensor in the corner of the conference room. The sensor's green LED light indicated that the alarm was actively protecting this zone of the law office.

Mack would have difficulty in getting into this office without being detected. He was sure that there were additional alarm sensors protecting the rest of the space. Even if he forced his way into the office, he would not be able to do so without alerting Quinn of his presence. In addition, Quinn was armed and knew how to use that weapon. Mack would have to plan his attack at a time when Quinn was leaving his office.

Mack's attention was broken by movement at the far end of the alley. Movement betrays even the most camouflaged target. He stopped looking through the window and walked towards the area where he saw the movement, all his senses tuned for a potential threat. The first step in neutralizing any threat is to recognize it. Mack changed his stride by walking more flat-footed, greatly decreasing the noise made by his heels and providing increased balance. As he exited the alley, he saw a man walking across the street and into another alley between two buildings. The man was dressed in dark clothes, wearing a dark colored leather jacket.

Mack crossed the street but did not follow the man down the alley. Instead, he continued past the alley and stopped a block down the street, finding a place in the shadows to hide. At this point, Mack didn't know what this person's intentions were. He knew that this man was armed, but he didn't know what he was doing in the alley. Mack dismissed the idea that this man was intending to commit a robbery. The man was dressed too well and had a professional look about him. Mack surmised that this man was a professional hit man. Several minutes later, the man exited the alley and looked around to see if he was being watched. The man, believing that he was not being observed, crossed the street and headed back towards the alley by the law office.

Mack followed at a safe distance, keeping in the shadows as much as possible. He knew that this man may not be alone, that someone else may be watching. He decided to keep his distance and see how things played out. Perhaps an opportunity would present itself.

Mack walked down the opposite side of the street and past the alley that he had just exited. He found a spot in front of a building that had an entrance where he could stand and watch the alley across the street without being seen. Mack saw a man looking into the same law office window that he had been looking through just moments before. The man had his hands cupped together with his face pushed up against the window. He wondered if this man was one of Rippy's Raiders. Mack dismissed the idea because Rippy's men always kept their distance from any intended target. Their surveillance was conducted at a safe distance. Rippy's men would have been using video equipment and would not be taking a risk of standing in a dark alley, peering into a small window.

Mack noticed that the light emanating from the law office conference room window went out. As soon as the light went out, the man looking through the window quickly left the alley and walked to a small parking lot at the rear of the law office building. The man hid in the shadows near where Quinn had parked his car. Mack could see the man crouched down, trying to hide himself from view. He was holding a handgun and was watching the back door of the law office building.

Quinn emerged from the rear door of the law office carrying a briefcase which was made to look like saddle bags. He was holding the briefcase in his left hand, allowing access to his six-shooter with his right hand. Quinn was dressed in black denim pants, black cowboy boots, a black leather vest, and a red shirt. On top of his head he wore a black cowboy hat with a straight brim. Around his waist, he wore a black leather gun belt with a silver six-shooter in the holster. Quinn looked like he walked right out of a western movie. The only thing missing was the jingling of spurs.

He was looking around for any potential threats. His nerves had been on edge since the day he was handed the note in court. He moved his hand towards his pistol, ready to draw in an instant.

As Quinn approached his car, the man stepped out of the shadows and approached him. Quinn immediately saw the man coming and drew his six-shooter from his holster with incredible speed. Mack was impressed with how quickly Quinn got the pistol out of his holster. The man raised a semi-automatic handgun and was able to get off one round before Quinn returned fire killing the man.

The impact of the bullet spun Quinn around. Quinn felt the searing pain as the bullet entered his body. He knew that the threats made against him were now being carried out. Unfortunately for Quinn, the man's bullet had struck him in his arm. His wound was not serious, but would require medical attention. Quinn's first reaction was to call the police, but needed to address any immediate threat before doing so. He didn't want to die holding his cell phone in his hand.

The sound of Quinn's six-shooter reverberated across the buildings. It was much louder than a normal handgun and Mack knew that the sound of gunfire would soon be bringing the police to the scene. He had fired in self-defense, but the attack on him had not yet ended. Quinn jumped in his car and pulled out of the parking lot. As he started to drive down the street, a black SUV emerged and slammed into Quinn's car. Quinn was forced off the road by the impact and crashed into a lamp post. Quinn quickly crawled across the front seat and exited the vehicle through the passenger side door.

The black SUV came to a screeching halt and two men exited and ran towards Quinn's car with guns drawn. Quinn had managed to make his way into a dark alley directly across from where his car crashed. The two men saw him enter the alley and followed him in. Mack knew that this action was not be a good idea. Quinn had the advantage, taking up a defensive position with a clear field of fire to the oncoming attackers.

Mack then heard the distinctive sound of Quinn's six-shooter. The bullet barely missed the two men, grazed off the side of the building before exiting the alley and whizzing past Mack's head. Mack instinctively hit the ground. As Mack lay on the ground he heard police sirens. As the police sirens grew closer, he heard more gun fire. Mack heard two more rounds from Quinn's six-shooter and the sound of multiple shots from the men's semi-automatic handguns.

Mack saw Quinn run from behind a building with the two men chasing him. He was amazed that no one got hit from all that gunfire. Quinn ran across the street, back towards where Mack was standing, the silver six-shooter shining from the light emitted by the street lights. Mack was still lying on the ground. Quinn ducked behind a parked car and shot at the two men as they crossed the street. Taking fire, the two men ducked and ran half-bent over to the other side of the street and took up positions about fifty yards from Quinn. Mack heard the shots ricocheting off the buildings down the street.

As a single police car arrived, the police officer saw Quinn shooting at the two men. The policeman yelled at Quinn to drop his weapon, but Quinn ignored the request. The policeman had his weapon drawn and was yelling again for Quinn to drop his weapon. Seeing that the police had Quinn engaged, the two men left their place of cover and ran back towards their black SUV. Quinn, still ignoring the policeman's request to drop his weapon, fired at the two men as they attempted to leave the scene. The policeman then fired one round at Quinn.

Quinn now realized that he was receiving fire from behind him. He turned around, weapon still in hand, and pointed it at the police officer. The police officer, responding to the threat, opened fire striking Quinn several times. Quinn slumped over, falling onto his side, the six-shooter still in his hand. The two men then ran back to their vehicle and departed the scene before the arrival of police backup.

Mack watched as the police officer approached Quinn and kicked the six-shooter out of his hand. Quinn was lying on the ground as the police officer rolled him onto his stomach and handcuffed him. By this time, the area was now crawling with police vehicles. Hearing all the excitement, a crowd of people had come out of the buildings and were being directed away as the police were putting up crime scene tape. Mack joined the crowd posing as a bystander.

Mack waited until the ambulance arrived and loaded Quinn in the back of the vehicle. The paramedics did not place him in a body bag, as he was still clinging to life. The ambulance departed the scene but did not activate its lights or siren. Mack noticed a mobile news crew showing up at the scene. Mack left the area before his picture in the crowd of bystanders wound up on the eleven o'clock news.

Mack walked back to his vehicle and drove slowly out of the area. If Quinn was dead, then his mission was completed. If Quinn was still alive, then his mission had failed, at least for now. Mack's next course of action depended on whether Quinn lived or died. He would watch the local news to learn the details of the incident he just witnessed. As he drove back to his hotel, he wondered what Rippy's reaction would be. If Quinn pulled through his injuries, Mack would have to wait weeks, if not months, to get another shot at Quinn. He put that thought out of his mind for the moment. His thoughts changed to the men outside of his hotel room.

Mack arrived at his hotel and pulled into the parking lot. He didn't park in the spot directly in front of his room. He wanted the men to see him walk across the parking lot and enter his room. Mack parked at the end of the parking lot near the hotel office. He went inside of the office and paid his room bill. He told the clerk on duty that he would be leaving in a couple of hours. Mack then walked to his room, acting as if he was inebriated. He walked with a limp and staggered as he made his way to the room. Most of the young men, who had been drinking, had already departed. However, the leader of these men was still on the second floor, drinking beer with two women.

As Mack got close to his room, the man began to taunt him again. Mack turned, looked at the man, and raised his middle finger. The man immediately became irate and started cursing at Mack. He ignored the man and opened the door to his room and stepped inside. Once inside, he took up a position behind the door. Mack heard footsteps approaching his room. The door burst open with a swift kick and a man rushed in, knife in hand, searching the room. Mack stepped from behind the door and elbowed him in the neck. The brachial stun dropped the man to his knees. While the man was trying to catch his breath, Mack grabbed his arm and twisted it into a wrist lock. Mack slammed the man's head into the dresser, rendering him unconscious. He tossed the man onto the bed and left the room.

Mack drove around the city looking for a place to get some dinner. He found a restaurant which claimed to have the best steaks in New Mexico. The bar was large, with more than thirty bar stools surrounding it. There were eight large screen televisions hanging above the bar, four on each side. He took a seat near one of the televisions. Bar patrons were playing trivia, answering their questions with an electronic device which recorded their responses.

Mack ordered a beer and asked to see a menu. He scanned the menu and ordered a steak and baked potato. As he waited for his food, the trivia game ended and the bartender changed the channel to the national news. Mack watched the news for any information about Quinn. The news didn't mention anything about New Mexico, rather just a bunch of pundits arguing about the president's policies and actions. When Mack's food arrived, the bartender asked Mack, and the other patrons at the bar, if he could change the channel to the local news. Receiving no objection, the bartender changed the channel.

The newscaster was reporting that at least one person was killed during a shooting which occurred earlier that evening. While details were still coming in, police observed one suspect shooting at two other suspects. Police demanded that the armed suspect drop his weapon and when the suspect refused and pointed his weapon at police, the police officer responded striking the suspect several times. The suspect was taken into custody and transported to a local hospital where he was listed in serious condition. Police are cautioning residents to stay indoors as police continue to search for the other two suspects. These suspects left the scene in a black SUV and are considered to be armed and extremely dangerous. Citizens are cautioned not to approach these men, but contact authorities immediately.

Mack thought that the news actually got it right this time. He did learn one additional detail. Quinn was in serious condition. It looks like Quinn was alive. Mack finished his meal and ordered another beer. He had nowhere to go. He already checked out of his hotel and didn't know where the mission would take him next.

When the bartender brought Mack his beer, the cell phone that Rippy provided started to ring.

"What's up?" Mack said into the phone.

"That's what I'd like to know," Rippy replied.

"You tell me. You got more information that I do," Mack said sternly.

"Quinn was the target of a mob hit. We didn't have the ability to stop it," Rippy said.

"So what now?" Mack asked.

"We'll have to wait and see what happens to Quinn," Rippy said. "Standby..." Rippy put Mack on hold. Mack considered hanging up, but Rippy would just call back. Rippy was back on the phone after a few moments.

"Quinn's condition has changed. We just got word from our person inside the hospital."

"Changed to what?" Mack asked, growing more impatient with each passing minute.

"Changed to deceased," Rippy said. "This mission is now complete. We'll be in touch with your next assignment. We will send it to you at the hotel."

"I'll let you know which hotel. Wasn't happy with the accommodations. Found a large cockroach in my room," Mack said.

"Let me know which hotel," Rippy said.

"Will do," Mack said as he hung up the phone. Mack had no intention of telling Rippy which hotel he would be staying at. Rippy would have to find out on his own.

Mack found a hotel near the airport and checked into his room. He threw his duffle bag on the bed and sat down in one of the chairs. He grabbed the remote control off the table and turned on the television, flipping through the channels until he found the local news. Just as Rippy had said, Quinn was dead. The newscast was showing a breaking news story. The reporter, an attractive young female, was providing the details. Mack turned up the volume on the television.

"Here's the latest on the shooting incident that has now left two people dead and two armed suspects still at large. The latest victim has been identified as Thomas G. Quinn, the flamboyant attorney who had gained national fame for his legal representation of organized crime figures. Sources close to the investigation tell us that Quinn succumbed to his injuries which resulted from a shoot-out with police. Sources indicate that Quinn was targeted by the same crime syndicate that he had been providing legal services to. The other victim in this case had connection to this very same criminal syndicate and was known on the street as a mob hit man. Investigators tell us that the mob hit man had been lying in wait for Quinn to exit his law office. An exchange of gunfire between Quinn and the hit man resulted in the mobster being killed and Quinn injured. Investigators are still trying to piece together why Quinn did not drop his weapon when ordered to do so by police. An unnamed source told News Six that Quinn had received death threats in the days leading to the assassination attempt. Police are asking anyone who witnessed the crime to contact them immediately."

Mack turned the television off. His sleep was interrupted by a knock on the door. Mack rose out of bed and looked through the door's peephole. A hotel employee standing in the hallway had a brown envelope in his hand. Mack opened the door slowly, only open enough to see who was standing on the other side.

"Mr. Brittan?" the hotel employee asked.

"Yeah, that's me. What's the problem?"

"No problem sir. A man just dropped this off at the front desk and asked that I give it to you," the man said holding the brown envelope out for Mack.

Mack opened the door wider and took the envelope.

"Wait one second, I'll give you something for your trouble," Mack said reaching for his wallet.

"No need sir. We're not allowed to accept tips," the man said turning to leave.

Mack held out a twenty-dollar bill. "I won't tell anyone."

"Thanks, but no thanks. It is part of the service we provide to our guests," the man said as he turned to walk down the hallway.

Mack shrugged and closed the door. He took the brown envelope over to the desk, turned on the light, and plopped down in the chair. This envelope was much thicker than the others. Mack manipulated the envelope without opening it, feeling for wires or explosive material that might be inside. While Mack didn't expect it to contain explosives, it was the unexpected that got people killed. Seven of the twelve targets had been eliminated. There were five left. Mack thought about eliminating Rippy now, but Candy was not in a safe position. He couldn't take any risk that she would be harmed. He would follow Rippy's orders until the appropriate time. At some point, Rippy would make an attempt on his life.

Mack opened the envelope carefully. The envelope was sealed across the back with brown packaging tape. He pulled out his lock blade knife and sliced the bottom of the envelope. If the envelope did contain explosives, the trigger would be located where the envelope was sealed and taped. Mack carefully opened the bottom of the envelope and looked inside. Seeing no wires or explosives, he removed the contents from the envelope. His next

156

target: *Edmond R. Watts—Selected for Termination for Crimes Committed against the United* States.

CHAPTER THIRTEEN

There was no mention of the specific crimes that Watts was alleged to have committed. Mack knew full well what "crimes" this man had done. He was a member of the "Ring of Twelve" and Rippy was systematically eliminating them one by one.

Watts was an arms dealer. Over the past several years, he had been selling weapons to the Mexican drug cartel. The weapons equipped the cartel with sufficient fire power to hold their own, even against the Mexican army. Murders were occurring almost on a daily basis in the border towns. Women and children were being killed as the ruthless drug cartel exacted its revenge on the society members who stood in its way. As the drug cartel's operations grew, so did their need for more weapons. Watts was more than happy to provide whatever they needed. He would sell arms to anyone willing to pay for them. There wasn't anything ethical or honorable about Watts. He was rotten to the core.

The dossier was filled with stack of photographs depicting Watts meeting with members of several drug cartels. Mack wondered why Rippy provided so many photographs of this target. Previous assignments only included a few photos. Mack studied each photograph carefully, memorizing the faces of everyone. Mack looked through the rest of the documents in the dossier. He learned that Watts had been traveling in and out of Mexico, crossing the border in El Paso, Texas.

El Paso has been engulfed in Mexican drug cartel violence that has spilled over into Texas. Nearly two thousand people have been killed in Juarez in the last three years. The violence started about the same time as Watts began selling weapons to the drug cartel.

The drug cartel's control of Juarez made it easy for Watts to smuggle his weapons across the border. Tractor trailers were rarely searched going into Mexico. Bribes and intimidation helped ensure that the containers filled with weapons were never searched.

Mack didn't find an airline ticket in the brown envelope. Instead, he was instructed to drive to El Paso. Mack grabbed his GPS out of his duffle bag.

Mack arose early the next morning and was eager to get on the road. After showering and getting dressed, he checked out of his room and helped himself to the complimentary continental breakfast. The morning newspaper, which was lying at his table, had Quinn's picture on the front page. The headline read: "*Mobster Lawyer Gunned Down by Police.*" The news article was almost a repeat of last night's newscast. He did learn one additional detail. The trial that Quinn was involved in was delayed. Since Quinn had been the lead defense attorney, the trial could not continue without him. The newly appointed defense attorneys were expected to motion for a mistrial, sending the case back to square one. Mack finished his breakfast and jumped into a 4x4 pickup truck which would blend in with the thousands of other pickup trucks down in El Paso.

Mack left Albuquerque and headed south on Interstate 25. Driving south, he wondered how he would terminate Watts. The dossier indicated that he traveled with heavily armed security personnel. He considered going into Mexico to eliminate the target, but that was not the ultimate solution. Mack spoke Spanish, but just enough to get by. He would be an outsider to both the drug cartel and the Mexican Army. His best chance of success would be to eliminate the target in El Paso. He remembered from the dossier that Watts had been providing weapons to drug cartels fighting each other for control of the drug enterprise.

Mack continued driving south past Truth or Consequences, a town which changed its name from Hot Springs to a popular 1950s game show. He continued past the White Sands Missile Range and Fort Bliss Military Reservation. At Las Cruces, the City of Crosses, he headed east onto Interstate 10 on his way into El Paso. Las Cruces had a place in old west history with tales of famous exploits by Billy the Kid and Sheriff Pat Garrett.

Mack located the hotel and pulled into the parking lot. He took a quick drive around the hotel's immediate vicinity, looking at the surrounding neighborhood. His experience with the last hotel Rippy provided was less than satisfactory. If he didn't like what he saw at this hotel, he wouldn't bother checking-in. The hotel appeared to be of newer construction. Mack decided that this hotel would be sufficient. He checked in and got the key to his room. The first thing that he noticed when he entered the room was a fresh, clean smell. The draperies were pulled open and the bright, Texas sun had warmed the room. The furniture was new and the bathroom modern. Mack had no sooner entered his room when the cell phone that Rippy provided started ringing. Mack grabbed the phone and answered it.

"Yeah, what's up? Mack said in his usual greeting to Rippy.

"I assume you read the dossier?" Rippy asked in his normal solemn tone.

"Cover to cover," Mack said.

"This is going to be your toughest assignment yet," Rippy replied.

"That's how I have it figured as well. May take several weeks, if not months, to complete." Mack knew this would irritate Rippy.

"We don't have months, or even weeks," Rippy said in an

irritated tone. "This needs to be accomplished in a matter of days."

"I'm open to suggestions," Mack said.

"I will provide whatever support you require."

"Let me give it some thought. I have a plan bouncing around in my head. Have someone else do the actual deed."

"I like the idea of having someone else do the actual deed. I will give it some thought also. I'll be in touch in a couple of hours," Rippy said as he hung up the phone.

Mack pulled out the dossier and spread the contents on his bed. There had to be an answer in all these documents. Mack looked at each document again, looking for any clue as to the best way to terminate Watts. Mack considered a sniper attack but dismissed that option for the present time. Watts traveled with heavy security and a failed sniper attack would make it much more difficult to get close enough to Watts to try a second attempt. Mack also considered a bomb, but there might be collateral damage to innocent people.

If he could convince the drug cartels that Watts was playing them against one another, Watts would be in a difficult predicament. Add in some "disinformation" that he is secretly working with the Mexican Army, the noose would draw even tighter around his neck. While it wasn't the perfect plan, it had the greatest probability of success. Rippy would be able to assist in the operation by helping to get the "disinformation" into the right hands. Mack gathered up the documents lying on the bed and placed them back into the brown envelope. He then laid down on the bed and took a nap, waiting for Rippy to call back. Perhaps Rippy had a better plan.

The ringing of the cell phone awakened Mack. He had been asleep for over two hours. On the fifth ring, the cell phone went silent. Mack closed his eyes and wanted to fall back asleep. He knew that he had better return Rippy's call or he would be calling again and again until Mack answered. Mack got out of bed, trying to chase the cobwebs from his mind. He picked up the cell phone and pulled up the missed call menu. He selected the last missed call and hit the "send" button. Rippy answered on the second ring.

"What have you come up with?" Rippy asked.

"If it needs to be done in a few days, it will have to be done by the cartels or the Mexican army," Mack said as he started to lay out his plan. "Watts is too well protected. His heavily armed security detail will make it nearly impossible to get close enough for a traditional attack. Explosives are another option, but the problem of getting close enough still remains. Even if we could get close enough to plant the explosive, the result of a bomb exploding in El Paso would bring unacceptable attention from other feds."

"Agreed," Rippy replied. "Your plan to involve the drug cartels or the Mexican army has merit. What do you suggest?"

"A disinformation campaign. We need to make the drug cartels believe that Watts is supplying weapons to all sides."

"That is already the case," Rippy explained. "He has been supplying the cartels with weapons for several years. He doesn't discriminate when it comes to selling arms. However, if I am correct, the cartels don't know that it is Watts who is supplying the other drug cartels."

"What about the Mexican army? Do they know Watts is involved in the supply of weapons to the drug cartels?"

"They've been suspicious for some time now. We have a contact inside the Mexican army. We can pass any information to him and it will be acted upon."

Mack thought to himself, if Rippy had evidence of Watts'

involvement with the illegal sale of arms, why hadn't he passed it along to the Mexican authorities? Mack knew the answer all too well.

"The dossier indicated that Watts would be delivering a large arms shipment to the Juarez drug cartel two days after tomorrow. We only have a day or so to set the stage for turning the cartels against Watts. I need to meet a member of the Juarez cartel tomorrow or the next day. I'll need a Russian passport and documents."

"I can create a Russian passport and papers by late tomorrow. I'll arrange for you to meet a member of the Juarez cartel. I assume that you will be traveling to Juarez?"

"No. The meeting must take place here in El Paso. For me to travel to Juarez with a Russian passport would raise a huge red flag to the Mexican border guards. They may be suspicious enough to detain me. Members of the cartel travel freely across the border. It won't raise any suspicion," Mack said.

"Understood," Rippy replied. "What information do you want me to pass to my contact in the Mexican army?"

"Pass along the date, time and location of the arms deal. Provide the photographs of Watts meeting with members of the Juarez drug cartel."

"How can we be sure that Watts will be killed?" Rippy asked.

"We can't be sure. It is what it is," Mack spouted.

"I'll do my part, Mack. The rest is up to you."

Mack hung up the phone and grabbed the dossier. He pulled out the photographs of Watts and destroyed the rest of the file.

Mack left the hotel and dove around El Paso looking for a place to hold the meeting with the cartel. He needed a place where he could see anyone approaching. That left the city a poor choice for the meeting. Mack drove out of the city and headed north on a road leading out of town towards White Sands Missile Range. A few miles out of town, Mack found a place off the highway, far enough away that it couldn't be seen from the road. This area provided a good viewpoint to observe the members of the drug cartel as they approached.

Mack drove back to his hotel room and waited for Rippy to create his passport and arrange the meeting.

Early the next morning, Mack heard a knock on his hotel room door. Mack crossed the room and looked through the peephole. Seeing no one, Mack opened the door slightly, leaving the chain on, and noticed a brown envelope lying on the floor. He grabbed it and closed the door. Mack sliced the envelope open with his lock black knife and pulled out a red passport with Russian Federation Passport embossed in gold lettering across the front in both Russian and English. The passport contained biometric data contained on a microchip embedded within the passport. Rippy has used Mack's driver's license photo, but the passport identified the man as Rostislav Andropov. Mack flipped to the last few pages. Immigration stamps indicated that Andropov had entered the U.S. two weeks ago in New York.

Mack had to hand it to Rippy. In only one day, he was able to create a Russian passport and immigration documents. Although these documents would not fool a Russian border guard, there were more than sufficient to fool a member of the Juarez drug cartel. Mack folded the immigration document and placed it inside the passport. He then removed all items from his wallet that identified him as Paul Brittan. Mack put his wallet back into his pocket and placed the passport in the inside pocket of a black, lightweight jacket. He also placed the photographs of Watts meeting with the

Mexican army in the same pocket. All that Mack needed now was the details for the meeting with the cartel. He didn't have to wait long.

"Yeah, what's up?"

"I take it that you received the package?" Rippy asked.

"I got it. Not bad forgeries."

"I have arranged for you to meet a senior member of the Juarez drug cartel. They insisted that the meeting take place in Juarez."

"Not possible," Mack said. "The meeting must take place in El Paso."

"Understood," Rippy said in his usual solemn tone. "After much discussion, I convinced them of the importance of the meeting and the need for it to take place in El Paso. They reluctantly agreed to meet you this afternoon."

"Set up the meeting for 3 O'clock. The meeting will take place outside the city in a remote location," Mack said.

"I'll pass the information along."

Mack gave Rippy the coordinates for the meeting location. Mack hung up the phone and looked at his watch. It was nearly 1:00 p.m. He needed to arrive at the predetermined site ahead of the cartel. He knew that the senior member would not be arriving alone. Mack put his pistol in his jacket pocket and slipped on the jacket. The cartel would most certainly search him, but a small pistol would not be a threat to the cartel.

Mack left the hotel and drove out to the site. He drove off the highway onto a dirt road which made its way up an incline about a quarter of a mile long. The road crested the hill and emptied into a small bowl shaped area large enough to fit several vehicles. Mack backed into a spot, facing his vehicle towards the road leading to the highway. Mack could not see the highway from his current position. There was only one way into this spot and that was down the dirt road.

Mack turned off the vehicle and rolled down the windows. It was hot outside and the vehicle soon warmed to an unpleasant temperature. Shortly before 3:00 p.m., Mack heard the distinctive sound of tires rolling across the stone road and started the vehicle for a quick escape. He watched as a black SUV crested the hill and rapidly approached his vehicle. Mack quickly placed his hand on his pistol and slammed the vehicle into gear. If the cartel had planned on attacking him, he was ready.

Just before a head-on collision, the SUV swerved and pulled in next to him. Instantly, two Hispanic men jumped from the vehicle. Within seconds, the two men positioned themselves on either side of Mack's vehicle. Mack didn't flinch. The man closest to Mack motioned for him to exit the vehicle. Mack put the vehicle in park and opened the door. As he got out of the vehicle, a man approached and reached out to search him. Mack grabbed the man's outstretched arm and twisted it into a wrist-lock causing the man to wince with pain and dropping to one knee. The other man reached for his own weapon, but before he was able to do so, Mack had his pistol drawn and was pointing it at the man.

"Don't even think about it!" Mack said forcefully in a Russian accent.

"Enough," a voice said from inside the black SUV. The man took his hand off his weapon and Mack released the other man's arm. A tall, Hispanic man, dressed in all black, matching his hair and several days' growth beard, exited the vehicle. Mack looked at the man's hands. He did not see a ring, nor had he really expected to see it. This man was the senior member of the Juarez drug cartel that he was scheduled to meet.

"You asked to meet. What do you want?"

"Business," Mack said in heavy Russian accent. "If you live to see another day."

"If I die, so do you!" the cartel member said angrily.

"I'm not here to kill you. If I had, you wouldn't be standing here talking to me," Mack said staring the man down.

"Get to the point," the cartel member shouted.

Mack reached inside his jacket pocket. Instinctively, the two security men reached for their weapons.

"Get your hands off those weapons," Mack shouted. "I'm pulling out some pictures." The two men did not comply with Mack's direction.

"Do as he says," the cartel member said in Spanish. Mack knew enough Spanish to understand what was said. The two men removed their hands from their weapons, but watched Mack very carefully, ready to draw their weapons at the first sign of trouble. Mack pulled out the photographs from his jacket pocket. He flipped through several photographs and handed one to the senior cartel member. The man looked at the photographs and then at Mack.

"How do I know this photo is real?"

"You don't," Mack said. "You'll have to trust me."

"Why should I trust you?"

"Because if you don't, you will be dead," Mack replied. "The end of the Juarez drug cartel would not be in either of our best interests."

"You got guts, I'll give you that," the cartel member said laughing. "Pictures can be fabricated. I need more proof than a couple of photographs."

Mack handed the cartel member the rest of the photos. The

man looked through the photos and his demeanor changed instantly.

"Where did you get these?"

"Not your business," Mack said. As soon as Mack said this, the two men drew their weapons and pointed them at Mack.

"Search him," the cartel member said. The man removed the passport and Mack's pistol from his jacket pocket. The man then handed the passport to his boss. The cartel member flipped through the passport, paying close attention to the immigration stamps at the back of the passport. The man handed the passport back to Mack.

"What about my pistol?" Mack asked.

"You'll get that back when our business is concluded. I'll ask you again, what is your business?"

"I've been sent here to conduct business. We will supply you with weapons. In return, you supply us with money and drugs," Mack said in his Russian accent.

"We already have a supplier," the cartel member said still looking at the photographs.

"Look to me like he supplies the Mexican army too," Mack said with a smirk. "Not to mention your rival cartels."

The man's face flashed with anger. The man kept staring at the photos of Watts, growing angrier with each passing moment. After a long pause, the man spoke.

"This pig," the cartel member said striking the photograph of Watts with his finger. "We suspected that he was working with our rival cartels, but we didn't suspect him of working with the Mexican army."

"You can take that up with him," Mack said. "We'll deal with him when the time comes. Russians have a way of dealing with traitors."

The Juarez cartel was considered one of the most ruthless criminal organizations operating in Mexico. Mack knew that implying they needed help, especially from the Russians, would be offensive.

"We don't need your help," the cartel member shouted. "You tell your bosses that we'll consider their offer. Next time we meet in Juarez."

The man holding the pistol started to hand it to Mack and then quickly tossed it in the air over Mack's head. Mack wanted to strangle the life out of this guy. The two men entered their black SUV after holding the door for their boss to enter. The driver quickly backed up the vehicle, sending stones and dust into the air. The SUV spun around and quickly accelerated over the crest of the hill.

Mack walked over and picked up his pistol from the ground and got into his vehicle. As he drove down the stone road, he saw the black SUV speeding away in the distance. Mack entered the highway, driving in the opposite direction, heading away from his hotel. He didn't want to head towards his hotel until he was sure that he wasn't being followed. He searched the sky for any sign of an aircraft or helicopter. Mack didn't see any indication of the authorities, but he still drove around for nearly an hour before returning to his hotel.

Mack entered his room and placed the documents identifying him as Paul Brittan back into his wallet. He checked the small, motion-operated video camera that he left in the room prior to his meeting with the drug cartel. The camera did not indicate any movement in the room while he was away. He was confident that no one had entered his room. Mack picked up the cell phone and called Rippy.

"How did the meeting go?" Rippy asked.

"As well as can be expected. The photographs had the desired result," Mack replied.

"What about Watts?" Rippy asked.

"I don't think the cartel is happy with him," Mack said sarcastically. "I'll think they'll take care of the issue. What we don't know is when or where."

"I'll arrange the when and where," Rippy stated.

"As we discussed, the Mexican army must not move in until the arms deal is completed," Mack reminded Rippy.

"Understood," Rippy said a little annoyed.

Mack hung up the phone. His part of the plan was complete. It was up to Rippy to get Watts to show up at the next day's arms deal. All that was left now was the waiting.

Rippy telephoned his contact in the Mexican army and reaffirmed that he knew the date, time and location of the pending arms deal. He also reminded them to not move in until the arms deal had been completed. Rippy then made a phone call to Watts.

"This is Watts."

"We have an issue," Rippy said. "I have information that the Juarez cartel is looking at conducting business with the Russian mob. We can't let them get a foothold into our operations."

"I don't believe that is the case," Watts said. "There's been no indication that the Russian mob is involved in supplying arms to the cartels."

"Then explain to me why a representative of the Russian mob met with a senior member of the Juarez drug cartel this afternoon in El Paso," Rippy said sternly.

"I'm in El Paso. If there was a meeting between the Russian

mob and the cartel, I would have known about it."

"Check your text messages," Rippy said. "Once you see the photos, call me back." Rippy then hung up the phone.

Watts noticed that he had several text messages. Watts opened the photos and saw Mack's earlier meeting. He immediately recognized the senior member of the Juarez cartel. Watts finished looking through the photos and called Rippy.

"You saw the photos?" Rippy asked.

"What are the Russians doing meeting with the Juarez cartel?"

"That's what I've been trying to tell you," Rippy said growing more annoyed. "Once they get a foothold in Mexico, we will never get them out. This is your problem. I expect you to deal with this personally."

"I'll take care of it. There's a transaction tomorrow in Juarez. I'll handle it personally."

"Fine, I expect this to be resolved." Rippy then hung up the phone.

Watts was angry. He regretted his association with Rippy. Rippy had taken control of his weapon shipment operations. Several years ago, Watts was a small-time dealer in illegal arm sales. He sold stolen weapons to whoever had the cash to pay for them. Things were going well for his criminal enterprise until one of the weapons he sold wound up in a school shooting where several students were killed. The Bureau of Alcohol Tobacco and Firearms was heavily involved in tracking down the individuals responsible for the sale of this particular weapon. Luckily for Watts, the ATF could not connect him to the sale of this weapon.

Watts thought he was home free until one day he was approached by a man claiming to have proof that he sold the weapon used in the school shooting. Watts denied he sold the weapon, but the man wrote the name of the person to whom Watts had sold the weapon on a piece of paper. Watts was astounded that this man was able to make the connection where the ATF had failed. Watts denied the allegation, but the man was not deterred. The man offered Watts a deal. Join the organization or the evidence would be turned over to the authorities. Watts, faced with no other option, reluctantly agreed.

Once a member of the organization, Watts' illegal arms sales took on a whole new life. The arms deals grew from a small operation into a large-scale enterprise involving world-wide criminal organizations. Watts had his greatest success in supplying weapons to the Mexican drug cartels. It was not uncommon for Watts to turn a profit of a million dollars on a single arms transaction. The profits were invested into both legitimate and criminal operations. Watts, like the rest of the members of the organization, was limited to the amount of money that he could withdrawal from the account for his personal use.

During the early stages of his involvement in the organization, Watts had asked for, and received, several large amounts of money. However, as time progressed, his requests were denied. Watts was angry that his requests were being denied given the large profits he was making for the organization. On one occasion, he expressed his growing dissatisfaction with Rippy, only to receive threats of retaliation if he stepped out of line. Watts had considered eliminating Rippy, but knew that if he failed, it meant certain death.

Watts began skimming some of the profits from the arms deal. He knew that small amounts were less likely to be noticed. He also purchased weapons with his own money and was selling them to the cartel in addition to the main shipments. What angered Watts the most was Rippy's control over him. He had to do what Rippy wanted, when Rippy wanted it. He wondered if Rippy had as much control over the other members of the organization. Little did he know that they were being systematically eliminated and he was the next target.

The next morning, Watts gathered his security detail and drove to the border crossing. He had already received word that the tractor-trailer had made its way across the border with the weapons undetected. Watts never felt comfortable traveling to Juarez. His security detail was unarmed. He couldn't take the risk of getting stopped by the U.S. Border Patrol prior to crossing the border. He had entered Mexico numerous times before unarmed, but this time he had an uneasy feeling about this trip. Rippy had been extremely terse with him the day prior. He couldn't afford to cross Rippy. He would meet with the cartel, resolve the issue with the Russian mob, and get back into Rippy's good graces.

Watts and his security detail crossed the border into Mexico without incident. The meeting with the Juarez cartel was arranged at a large warehouse facility on the outskirts of the city. Watts had been to this particular location on only one prior occasion. The arms transactions were rarely held in the same location and on several occasions, the location of the meetings were changed numerous times prior to the actual time. This was to keep the Mexican army off-guard and continually guessing as to the exact location of the meetings.

As Watts approached the warehouse facility, he noticed an unusual number of armed men surrounding the entrance to the complex. He did not see the tractor-trailer containing the weapons, but this was not out of the ordinary. The truck would have been pulled inside the building upon its arrival. The warehouse was rundown, typical of most buildings in Juarez. It had rained earlier in the day and the area in front of the warehouse was filled with puddles. Watts told his driver to pull up to the front of the building. As soon as the vehicle stopped, Watts exited from the back seat. He directed his security detail to remain in the vehicle, telling them that he would be returning in a short while.

Watts walked to the entrance of the warehouse where two members of the Juarez cartel were positioned on either side of the doorway. As he got closer to the entrance, both men pointed their weapons at Watts, indicating for him to stop. One of the guards motioned for Watts to put his hands in the air. Watts did as requested while the other guard approached him and conducted a pat-down inspection for weapons. Finding no weapons, the guards let Watts pass and enter into the building.

The entryway was dimly lit and it took a few moments before Watts' eyes adjusted to the darkness. He could make out two more armed guards standing on either side of a long hallway which lead into the main part of the warehouse. Watts walked past the two guards and down the long hallway. Watts reached a steel door and turned the knob. It was locked. Watts rapped twice on the door and waited for a response. The uneasy feeling he had prior to crossing the border returned, this time more intensely. He was at the complete mercy of the Juarez cartel. He needed to pull himself together. If he showed fear, the cartel would become suspicious. He had been careful not to let the cartels know that he was supplying weapons to all sides.

Watts pounded on the door again, this time the sound echoing down the long hallway. Within a few seconds, the door opened. Watts could see the main portion of the warehouse. The inside was lit with large mercury-vapor lamps suspended from the ceiling.

The lights were very bright and it hurt one's eyes to look directly at them.

The tractor-trailer was parked in the center of the warehouse with the back of its trailer doors swung open. A set of metal stairs was attached to the back of the trailer and armed guards were traveling up and down the stairs unloading the cargo. The guards were placing the weapons, including submachine guns and semi-automatic pistols, on long wooden tables. Men were seated behind the tables and were inspecting each weapon as it was placed in front of them. There were over two hundred rifles and a hundred handguns in this shipment. The cartel was inventorying each weapon, cross-referencing it to the order listing. Watts saw the senior cartel member sitting at a small table near where the weapons were being unloaded. Watts gave the man a quick smile, but the man turned away in the opposite direction. Watts walked over to the table and spoke to the man.

"Everything in order?"

"Not yet. Everything will be in order once we deal with a traitor."

"Traitor?" Watts asked sensing something was terribly wrong.

"Someone has been selling us out to the Mexican army."

"Any idea who?"

"We know exactly who," the man said looking directly at Watts.

Watts suddenly felt weak in the knees. His heart was pounding like a jackhammer in his chest. He felt a cold chill come across his entire body.

"What are you talking about? You don't think that...you think that I've been selling you out to the Mexican army?" Watts said with a slight stutter.

"Photos don't lie," the man said.

"Photos? What photos?"

The man removed the photographs of Watts meeting with the Mexican army and laid them on the table facing him. Watts immediately recognized himself in the photo meeting with a general in the Mexican army. Several months ago, Rippy instructed him to meet the general to discuss the interdiction of weapons being smuggled into Mexico. Rippy directed Watts to pose as a federal agent and obtain information regarding the tactics and strategies used to combat the illegal flow of weapons into Mexico. Watts had not been successful, the army refusing to devolve their tactics. Watts now knew that Rippy had arranged the meeting for the sole purpose of obtaining these photographs.

"You don't understand," Watts said in a panic state. "I met with them to learn their tactics and strategies to use against them."

"They know who you are," the man shouted. "We can't take that risk anymore."

Watts knew that fear was weakness. Perhaps if he stood up to these men, he could convince them. He had nothing to lose.

"You're wrong," shouted Watts. "I'm no traitor. Why would the Mexican army allow me to sell you weapons that would ultimately be used against them? It doesn't make sense."

"You sell weapons to our enemies. That makes you a traitor."

"I never sold weapons to the Mexican army. Why would they need to buy weapons from me? They can buy weapons from anyone in the world."

The man then placed the photographs of Watts meeting with the rival cartels on the table. Watts looked at the photographs and his heart sank. He might be able to talk his way out of the meeting with the Mexican army, but he had no chance of explaining away his dealings with the rival cartels. What he feared most was now happening. He had been caught playing both sides.

"You deny selling weapons to our enemies?" the man asked rhetorically.

Watts did not respond. There was nothing that he could say to refute the evidence in front of him. Desperation sank in. He would need to offer the cartel something extremely valuable to save his life.

"Keep the weapons. No charge."

"We already have them. What makes you think that we are going to pay for them?" the man said laughingly.

"I can get you whatever you need. Without me, you won't have a weapons supplier."

"We have a new weapons supplier. We don't need you anymore."

"You're being played," Watts said. "You didn't meet with the Russian mob. Let me guess, he's the one who gave you the pictures, right?"

"How do you know I met with the Russian?" The man's face flashed with anger. Suspicion now crept into his mind. Someone was setting Watts up, and he had a good idea who that was. It had to be the man he met claiming to be from the Russian mob.

"The leader of my organization told me yesterday that the Russian mob was trying to take our business. He told me to remedy the situation personally. That is why I am here."

"That still doesn't explain your dealing with our enemies," the man said pointing at the pictures of Watts with the rival cartels.

"I do as I'm told. I am the middle man in these transactions. I have no say to whom the weapons are sold. I am like you … a soldier following orders."

"Don't compare yourself to me," the man said rising from the table and pointing his finger at Watts. "You are no soldier."

The next thing Watts heard was the sound of gunfire. At first he didn't believe what he was hearing, but there was no mistaking the sound of automatic weapons fire. A major gun battle was occurring outside the warehouse. As Mack had instructed, the Mexican army was closing in on the cartel. Outside of the warehouse, Mexican forces had attempted to apprehend the cartel members located outside of the building, but the situation soon escalated into a major firefight. Although heavily armed, the cartel was no match for the Mexican army's firepower and armored vehicles.

Watts heard shouting and more gunfire. The shouting was coming from the Mexican soldiers instructing the cartel to put their weapons down. In all the confusion, Watts decided he would make a break for it. Watts took off running across the warehouse, looking for a place to escape. The only exit was through the steel door that he entered. As he approached the door, he felt a sharp pain in his side. He had been shot. He struggled to open the steel door, but it was locked and he was losing strength. As he turned, he saw the cartel member standing beside him.

"Traitor. You brought the Mexican army here."

A shot rang out, and as Watts went down, he yelled, "Rippy! Rippy!"

"What's a Rippy?" the cartel member asked the man next to him, who shrugged his shoulders.

Then an explosive charge blew the steel door off its hinges and the Mexican army charged in. The cartel members threw their weapons down and raised their hands. The battle was over.

Mack waited in his hotel room for word from Rippy. The arms deal was scheduled for 3:00 p.m. and it was now more than two hours after the scheduled meeting time. Mack laid down on the bed and closed his eyes. He thought about Candy. He made up his mind that he would visit her before the next mission. He didn't care what Rippy would say. He needed to know that she was safe. More importantly, he needed to be with her. He needed to keep her close in order to protect her.

CHAPTER FOURTEEN

Mack's thoughts were interrupted by the ringing of his cell phone. It was Rippy.

"Yeah, what's up?"

"The mission is complete," Rippy said in his usual solemn tone.

"The plan worked?" asked Mack.

"Indeed. In addition to the death of Watts, the Mexican army arrested a senior member of the Juarez cartel and numerous others. They also recovered over three hundred weapons."

"Then my part is finished," Mack said.

"Correct. Well done. We will send you the next information soon."

Within an hour, Mack received a phone call from the front desk. He took the envelope back to his room, scanned the outside of the envelope, and felt for wires or explosives before slicing it open with his knife.

Along with the dossier on his next target, Mack found an airline ticket. The flight was for the next day, a one-way ticket from El Paso to Baltimore. Mack knew that Candy was probably still located in Frederick, Maryland just a short drive from Baltimore. He needed to stay focused on the mission, but he couldn't help but consider a little detour. Mack pulled out the dossier and looked at the top page.

Vincent Bruno: Selected for Termination for Crimes Committed Against the United States.

The only crime Mack was aware that Bruno had committed was being a member of the "Ring of Twelve". Mack looked at the photographs. Bruno was in his late fifties or early sixties and was of Italian descent. His face was round and he wore designer glasses with the initials *VB* embossed in gold lettering on the sides. His black hair was combed straight back.

Mack learned that Vincent Bruno went by the nickname Vinny. Bruno operated a gentlemen's club in Baltimore named the "Shoe Store". The dossier indicated that Bruno spent most of his time at the club which was attached to a small strip mall. Bruno owned the other businesses in the mall including a gun shop with an indoor firing range. The club was located outside of the city in an area known for its high crime rate. Baltimore had a high homicide rate, ranking fifth in the nation.

Mack read the rest of the dossier and packed his belongings in preparation for the next day's flight. If possible, he would make it look like an accident. More preferably, he would have someone else do it for him. Mack knew too well that his missions were not sanctioned by the U.S. Government. Rippy had been using him to eliminate the other members of the organization. Mack struggled with the idea of continuing the mission. He had been duped into committing murder. Nothing he could do would change that. Perhaps he could at least rid society of these menaces.

Eight of the twelve targets had been eliminated. Osterman, Muhler, Rutherford, Samuels, Steiger, Black, Quinn, and Watts. Bruno was the ninth target. If Mack was correct, Rippy was the twelfth member. Mack figured that one of the twelve would not be a member of the "Ring of Twelve" or Rippy had purposely given Mack false information. Mack was betting on the latter. Rippy was a master of deception.

The next morning, Mack boarded the flight to Baltimore. Mack took the newspaper offered by the flight attendant and flipped through the pages. He pulled out his smart phone and typed a text message to Candy.

"Arriving Baltimore. 4 p.m. Wanna get together?"

Mack sent the message and flagged down the flight attendant. He ordered two beers. For Mack, a couple of beers made the flight more bearable. He was getting ready to turn off his phone for the flight to Baltimore when he received a text message. It was from Candy. Mack opened the text message and a large smile crossed his face.

"Paul. I miss you so much. Let me know the second you land. I'm still in the same hotel. Can't wait to see you."

Mack turned off his phone and sat back for the long flight into Baltimore. He drank his two beers and browsed through the newspaper. On the second page, an article caught Mack's attention. The article described a major advancement in Mexico's fight against the drug cartels. Mexican authorities conducted a raid in Juarez, capturing numerous members of the drug cartel and recovering hundreds of stolen weapons. Authorities report an American citizen was killed in the raid. He is believed to have been working with the drug cartel. Mack closed the newspaper and placed it in the seat back pocket in front of him. He closed his eyes and fell asleep. When he awoke, the plane was on final approach into Baltimore. He had been asleep for over four hours.

As the plane taxied to the gate, Mack turned his phone on. He sent a text message to Candy telling her that he just landed and would be seeing her soon. Almost instantly after he sent the message, he received a text message back from Candy.

"143?" Mack thought. "What the heck is that?"

Mack picked up his duffle bag at the baggage claim terminal. As instructed, he found a vehicle in the parking garage. This time, it wasn't a 4x4 pickup truck or SUV. Rippy had provided a dark colored sedan. As Mack approached the door of the vehicle, the doors automatically unlocked. He had heard that these type of vehicles only required the operator to have the key on their person. Mack opened the door and threw his duffle bag on the back seat. Mack pushed the start button and the car roared to life. In the center of the dash, Mack noticed a large LCD display. He pushed the button marked "Camera" and the screen depicted a 360 degree view of the outside of the vehicle. Mack noticed a button labeled "IR" and pushed it. An infrared image now appeared. *This was something out of James Bond*, Mack thought. He might be able to use this advantage during the next mission.

Mack drove out of the airport and headed towards Frederick. On the way to Candy's hotel, he stopped and bought a dozen red roses and two six-packs of beer. The closer he got to the hotel, the greater the anticipation grew inside of him. Mack flipped the console display screen to the GPS mode and typed in the hotel address. Although he knew where the hotel was located, he didn't want to delay his arrival, even by one minute. The GPS indicated the time of arrival in 39 minutes. Mack sent a text message to Candy.

"Arriving in 39 minutes." Mack sent the message and waited for a reply. In less than a minute, he received a text message from Candy.

"Be in your arms in 38 minutes."

Mack laughed at the response. He accelerated and the vehicle started to race. So did his heartbeat. He was excited. It was a great feeling. *So this is what life is like?* Mack thought to himself. Just as the GPS calculated, Mack arrived on time. As he drove into the parking lot, he looked at the window of Candy's room. Candy was standing by the window waiting for him to arrive. Mack parked the car and grabbed his duffle bag, roses and beer. As he walked across the parking lot, he looked up at Candy's room. She was waving wildly, trying to get his attention. Mack waved back and saw that beautiful smile on Candy's face. She turned away from the window and started down to the hotel lobby. As Mack got into the lobby, the elevator door opened and Candy emerged.

"Paul," Candy said running to greet him. As she reached him, she threw her arms around him nearly knocking him to the ground. Mack tried to return her embrace, but it was not easy carrying the duffle bag and flowers. Candy gave Mack a passionate kiss and his entire body start to tingle.

"I missed you so much, Paul. Did you miss me?"

"Give me a chance to put these things down and I'll show you just how much," Mack said with a wide grin.

Candy's face lit up like a small child on Christmas morning. Mack handed her the roses and guided her to the elevator with his arm around her lower back. As they entered the elevator, he whispered into Candy's ear.

"I've missed you. Did you miss me?"

Candy nodded agreement. Once inside the room, Mack pulled up the application on his smart phone that detects video signals. As Candy put the beer in the refrigerator, Mack scanned the signals and determined that Rippy had not placed any additional cameras in Candy's room.

"How about a beer?" Mack asked.

"Already got them ready," Candy said handing Mack a beer.

Mack took the beer from Candy as she sat down on the couch next to him. Mack could smell Candy's perfume. Candy had on a very form fitting, grey knit dress that accented her body very nicely. She put her hand on Mack's leg and Mack felt a warm sensation come over his body. He wanted her in the worst way. He placed his hand on Candy's thigh and she placed her hand on top of his. Candy started to rub Mack's hand which increased his desire for her.

"I need a shower," Mack said looking into Candy's bright blue eyes.

"Me too," Candy said moving Mack's hand higher up on her thigh.

Candy led Mack by the hand to the bathroom. Once inside the bathroom, Candy slipped out of her dress revealing her hard, athletic body. Mack quickly undressed and stepped into the shower with Candy following close behind. Mack embraced Candy, holding her tight against him. She began kissing his neck, her firm body tight against his. Mack whispered into her ear.

"I want you now."

"I'm all yours," Candy whispered back.

Mack turned off the shower and followed Candy into the bedroom. Mack closed the bedroom door for an afternoon of pure pleasure.

After a round of extreme passion, Candy fell asleep curled up next to Mack. He had never felt this good in his life before, except when he was with Candy. He fell asleep to the sound of Candy snoring ever so quietly. When he awoke, Candy was already out of bed. He was surprised that he did not wake up when she left the bed. He was usually a very light sleeper, conscious of every noise and movement. He could not remember a time when he had slept so deeply, except when he was a very young child. Mack felt refreshed, both physically and emotionally. He took a quick shower and got dressed. He found Candy in the kitchenette cooking breakfast. Mack smelled the familiar aroma of pancakes and bacon. It smelled wonderful.

"Morning sunshine," Candy said when Mack entered the kitchenette. "Sleep well?"

"Like a baby," Mack said as he kissed Candy on the neck.

"Me too."

Candy was wearing a pink sleep shirt and had her hair pulled back into a pony tail. The sleep shirt was barely long enough to cover her bottom. Even in this attire, she looked like a goddess. Mack thought how lucky he was to be with her. He was looking forward to finishing this whole ordeal with Rippy and hopefully being with her every day. He had a long way to go and the toughest parts still lay ahead. He knew that at some point Rippy would be coming after him. Mack was looking forward to the opportunity.

Mack ate the breakfast. He enjoyed the pancakes and bacon immensely. He never cooked for himself, choosing to eat out or throwing something in the microwave. This simple breakfast that Candy made, rivaled anything he had ever had. It wasn't the food that made the meal so delicious, but the fact that it was made by someone who truly cared for him. Mack watched as Candy ate her breakfast, cutting her pancakes into tiny pieces before eating them. She couldn't stop smiling at Mack.

"Any plans for today?" Candy asked with a wink and a smile.

"I need to go to Baltimore later tonight. I have a business meeting with a client at a club."

"Sounds like fun. Can I go?"

"Well, it's more of a club for men," Mack said as his face started to blush.

Candy saw the expression on his face and immediately knew what he was talking about.

"You would rather that I not go along?" Candy asked teasingly.

"You're welcome to come along. I just thought that it wouldn't be something that you would enjoy," Mack said not looking at Candy.

"I've seen it before," Candy said. "I'll go anywhere with you."

Mack's face turned red with embarrassment. He had hoped to find a way to take Candy to the strip club. He could use her in this mission. He didn't know how to ask her, but now the issue was on the table and she was a willing participant.

"Excellent. We'll make a night of it. I owe you a dinner for this excellent breakfast you made."

"Deal, and I know exactly what I want for dessert," Candy said with a wink and a smile.

"Me too," replied Mack.

"I'm going to take a bubble bath. I need someone to wash my back."

"I got your back," Mack said figuratively and literally.

Mack followed Candy into the bathroom and watched her as she filled the large bathtub with warm water. The tub was soon filled with lots of bubbles that smelled like vanilla birthday cake. Mack looked at the bottle of bubble bath and was not surprised that the fragrance was "Vanilla Birthday Cake". He was amazed how realistic the scent was. As Candy lay in Mack's arms, he thought about the current mission. He knew that Bruno owned and operated "The Shoe Store" gentlemen's club which was involved in prostitution and the illegal sale of narcotics.

Mack's plan was to visit the strip club and conduct some surveillance. If he went alone, he would not have much of a chance to meet Bruno. However, with Candy, he was sure to attract

Bruno's attention. The results of the night's trip to the club would determine how Mack would complete this mission. He needed to go shopping. Mack wanted Bruno to believe that he was extremely wealthy. The car Rippy provided would help create that illusion. Mack told Candy that he needed to go shopping and she was more than eager to go along.

Mack and Candy finished their bath and got dressed. Mack could still smell the bubble bath fragrance on his skin. He put on some men's body spray which covered up the vanilla birthday cake scent. At Mack's suggestion, Candy styled her hair and put on more makeup then she usually wore. Candy was beautiful without makeup, which Mack knew was the real sign of beauty. As Candy got ready, Mack sat on the couch and memorized the information in the dossier. After forty-five minutes, Candy emerged from the bedroom. Mack could not believe his eyes. Candy was even more beautiful than he had ever seen her. The blue eye shadow made her blue eyes look like diamonds floating on tropical waters. The lipstick accented her lips, enhancing her dynamite smile. Candy put the same grey knit dress back on that she wore the day before. She knew that Mack really liked this dress.

Mack and Candy jumped in the car and headed out to the mall. The first stop was to purchase new clothes for Mack. Mack never wore expensive clothes and was not "fashion-wise". Candy selected several outfits for Mack to try on. *Outfits?* Mack thought. *First a bubble bath and now trying on outfits?* Mack thought he would have to turn in his man card if this behavior continued. After several clothes changes, Mack settled on some designer shoes, shirt, pants, and belt. Now it was Candy's turn. Candy found a black, strapless sequin dress and shoes that matched. Mack paid for the clothes using Rippy's credit card. He then located an upscale jewelry store and purchased Candy diamond earrings, bracelet, and necklace.

Mack and Candy returned to the hotel and changed into their new clothes. Mack slipped on his Rolex submariner watch and placed a large roll of hundred-dollar bills in his pocket. Candy slipped into her new outfit and looked like a million dollars. The first part of the plan was now complete.

After eating at a fine restaurant, Mack drove to the gentlemen's club. Just inside the entrance, a man was collecting cover charges from entering patrons. As Mack pulled out his large roll of cash, the man collecting the cover charges spoke.

"You with her?" the man said pointing at Candy.

"Yeah. Is there a problem?"

"No problem. No cover charge for ladies."

Mack was about to pay his cover charge when the man held up his hand.

"You're good. As long as you're with her, no cover charge."

Mack thanked the man and found a booth along the back wall of the club. Mack slid into the booth with Candy right behind him. The club was dimly lit around the edges, the brightest lights shining on the center stage. On stage, a young, dark haired woman was dancing, twisting, and gyrating to the music. She was totally naked except for a pair of high-heeled shoes. Mack looked at Candy who was watching the girl dance. She turned, looked at Mack, and smiled. A young, blonde waitress dressed in a skimpy black bikini arrived at the booth and asked to take their drink orders. Mack ordered a beer and Candy ordered a vodka-cranberry cocktail. Mack could not help notice the voluptuous blonde waitress. She was very attractive. The woman flashed Mack a smile. Mack then felt Candy's hand upon his thigh.

"She's very pretty," Candy said.

"If you like that kind of stuff," Mack said.

"She definitely likes you."

"I have that effect on women," Mack said teasingly.

The waitress returned with the drinks and Mack pulled out his large roll of money. The waitress immediately noticed the large sum of money. Mack stripped off a hundred-dollar bill and gave it to the waitress. As she was counting out the change, Mack told her to keep it. She thanked Mack with a huge smile and walked over to one of the bouncers and motioned in Mack's direction. The bouncer walked across the club and entered a door leading to a small hallway. After a few minutes, the bouncer reappeared and talked to the waitress. The waitress returned to Mack's table carrying a bottle of expensive champagne.

"Compliments of the management."

"Tell them thanks," Mack said.

The waitress then slipped Mack a napkin which had her name and phone number written on it. The waitress gave make a wink and left the table. Mack looked at the napkin and handed it to Candy. Candy looked at the napkin and gave Mack a smile.

"Makes me want you even more," Candy said.

"I wouldn't trade you for all the money in the world," Mack said honestly.

Mack poured the champagne and handed a glass to Candy. "To us."

"To us," Candy said as the tears welled in her eyes. "I've never been this happy in my life."

"143," Mack said.

"I love you too."

Three men dressed in suits approached their table. The man in the middle was Vinny Bruno. As they made their way to the table, Bruno chatted with some of the patrons. When he got to Mack's table the other two men stood behind Bruno. Mack noticed the slight bulges in their suit jackets.

"Enjoying the champagne?" Bruno asked.

"Very much so. I'm Paul Brittan," Mack said reaching out to shake Bruno's hand, noticing the distinctive golden ring he wore.

"Vinny Bruno…and this lovely lady is?"

"Candy."

"So, what do you think of my club?"

"Very upscale. Why do you call it The Shoe Store?"

"Because that's all the girls on stage wear," Bruno said with a laugh. "Why don't you two be my guests in our VIP lounge?"

"Whatcha think?" Mack asked Candy.

"Why not?"

Mack and Candy left their booth and followed Bruno to the VIP lounge. The lounge was separate from the rest of the club and more elegantly furnished. Bruno took a seat in one of the booths which encircled an elevated dance stage. Mack and Candy sat down next to Bruno.

"What's your pleasure?" Bruno asked Candy.

"Champagne would be nice."

Bruno motioned for a waitress to bring a bottle of champagne.

"What about you, Paul?"

"I'll have champagne too."

The waitress brought a bottle of champagne and poured three glasses.

"What brings you to my club?"

"Business and pleasure," Mack replied.

"Business?" asked Bruno.

"I'm looking for some high-class talent. My clients are always interested in obtaining the absolute best."

"I may have some talent for you," Bruno said pointing at the dancer who just entered the stage. A stunningly beautiful girl dressed in a red thong bikini started dancing to the music. As she danced to the music, Mack watched more intently. He could feel Candy watching him, so he placed his hand on her thigh. Candy began rubbing his hand. Mack glanced at Candy and she too was watching intently.

"Whatcha think?" Bruno asked.

"Top notch," replied Mack.

"Perhaps we can do business then."

Mack looked at Bruno's left hand and noticed that he was wearing that distinctive ring.

"I think it's a good possibility. I'll give you thirty percent."

"Thirty? That's hardly worth my while. Alexis can bring in a couple of grand a week here. How about fifty?"

"I'm taking all the risk. My clientele pay extremely well. Thirty percent will greatly increase your profit margin."

Bruno thought about it for a second and then made a counter-offer. "Forty."

Mack appeared to be considering the offer and let Bruno sweat it out for a long minute.

"Okay, forty percent."

Bruno was elated. "Now that the business is completed, how about some pleasure?"

"I've got my pleasure right here," Mack said putting his arm around Candy.

Bruno handed Mack a business card. "My private number. Call me when you're ready to start." Bruno got up from the booth and walked to the door. "Enjoy yourselves," he said as he left the lounge.

Mack and Candy were now alone in the VIP lounge except for the dancer. They watched the girl dance, sipping on the champagne. Mack knew that the lounge was probably being watched through surveillance equipment. He also knew that the mirror directly behind them on the wall was two-way. The mirror was set into the wall and not mounted flush against it. Mack also noticed a change in the reflection of the mirror, indicating that someone was watching from the other side.

"She's going to make me a lot of money," Mack said.

"She got all the right moves," Candy said.

Bruno was watching Mack and Candy through the two-way mirror from a small room located on the other side of the wall of the VIP lounge. He was able to listen to Mack and Candy's conversation from the microphones located under the booth table.

"You run the plates?" Bruno asked one of his security guards.

"Yep. Car is a rental. We found out it was rented from BWI airport yesterday by Paul Brittan."

"Good work. Follow then and see where they go. I want to know everything that you can find out on this guy."

Mack and Candy left the lounge and walked to their car. Mack knew that they were being watched. Mack opened the car door for Candy. He then go into the car and started it up. He switched on the car's camera system and flipped the image to infrared. Mack could see a figure of a man hiding in the darkness at the far end of the club. As Mack put the car in gear, the man walked quickly to a vehicle and got inside. Mack pulled out of the parking lot and switched the camera view to the rear.

As he drove away, he could see a vehicle following him. Mack made a few quick turns to confirm he was being followed. The car behind him made the same turns, following at a close distance. Mack quickly accelerated, creating as much distance between himself and the car behind him. He switched the vehicle's camera to forward view, infrared mode, and turned off his headlights. The video image made it very easy to see without the headlights. He made a few more quick turns and stopped short of the intersection of the road he just came down.

In a few seconds, the car that had been following him barreled past his location at a high rate of speed, attempting to catch up. Mack waited as the car went past and then continued on. Mack entered the highway, turning in an opposite direction. After driving a short distance with the headlights off, he turned them back on. He had lost the vehicle. Mack drove back to the hotel and parked the car in a spot where it couldn't be noticed.

Mack and Candy went up to their room. Mack grabbed a beer out of the refrigerator and offered Candy one. She accepted the beer and took a seat on the couch. Mack took a seat beside her.

"Thanks for a wonderful evening, Paul."

"My pleasure. Thanks for going along."

"I enjoyed it immensely. Especially the club," Candy admitted.

Mack gave Candy a puzzled look. "You really enjoyed the club?"

Candy's face began to turn red. He could tell that she was embarrassed by her admission.

"I didn't think I was going to enjoy it, but seeing you watch that girl dance was...well...hot."

"As long as were being honest, watching her dance was hot, but not about her. The longer I watched, the more my desire grew for you," Mack said.

"You're so sweet. So, how about some dessert?"

Mack smiled and led Candy into the bedroom.

The next morning, Mack called Bruno and arranged for Alexis to meet a client at a Baltimore hotel. Bruno said that Alexis would be at the hotel at 7 p.m. Mack found a luxury hotel and made the room reservation. A couple of hours before the scheduled meeting time, Mack and Candy drove to the hotel. Mack checked in and got the key to the room. Candy and Mack then took the elevator to the top floor. He had reserved the best room in the hotel. As Mack entered the room, he was impressed. The entrance to the foyer was lined with Italian marble. The living room was large and inviting. Just off the living room there was a formal dining room that led into a large kitchen. Each of the two bedrooms had gas fireplaces and attached bathrooms with large whirlpool tubs.

Mack phoned Bruno and told him the room number. Bruno said that he would ensure that Alexis received the message. Shortly before 7 p.m., Mack heard a knock on the door. As Candy got up off the couch to answer it, Mack motioned for her to stay where she was. Mack wanted to make sure that it was safe. As he was walking towards the door, Candy got his attention and pointed at the television screen. As Candy was flipping through the channels, she came across a video image of the outside of their room door.

Mack recognized Alexis, but he didn't recognize the man that she was with. Mack had not expected Alexis to arrive with someone else, especially a man. Mack opened the door to let Alexis inside. Alexis gave Mack a huge smile and stepped inside. The man with her tried to enter, but Mack blocked his path.

"What's the deal?" Mack asked.

"Just need to make sure that it's safe."

"Safer than you think. You can wait in the hallway."

"You hurt her, and you'll deal with me."

Mack closed the door in the man's face. Alexis was already in the living room talking with Candy. Alexis was complimenting Candy on her outfit and shoes. Mack joined the two women in the living room.

"Would you like something to drink?"

"No thanks. Maybe later," Alexis said.

"Our client will be arriving in a short while. I'm responsible for handling all the details. You'll be paid five grand at the conclusion of the act."

"What act?" asked Alexis.

"Nothing perverted. Just straight sex."

"Sex? Mister, I'm a dancer, not a porn star."

"Why did you think you were coming here? For a five grand lap dance?" Mack acting greatly annoyed.

"Vinny sent me here. He told me to make the client happy. I told him that as long as that was getting naked and dancing then fine, but nothing more."

"And he sent you anyway?"

"He threatened me. He told me to make the client happy or I'll regret it. I can deal with Vinny. If I can't, my boyfriend can."

"You mean the guy in the hallway?"

"Yeah, he's not afraid of Vinny. If Vinny lays one finger on me, he'll be the one regretting it."

"You tell Vinny that he cost me a lot of money. Tell him our deal is off."

Mack walked Alexis to the door. He had a sudden dislike for her. He knew that she had come to the hotel hoping to bilk some guy out of thousands of dollars. She was quite the looker, but she had no class. Mack opened the door and let her out of the room. Mack closed the door and placed his ear against it to listen.

"That was quick," the man said.

"They wanted sex. I said no…they threw me out."

"How much did they offer?"

"What do you mean, how much?" Alexis said giving him a look that said it all.

Mack laughed to himself. He relayed the story to Candy and they both started laughing hysterically.

"There's no client coming, is there?" Candy asked.

"No."

"What type of business are you in? Are you a pimp?" Candy was clearly irritated.

"No. I make arrangements for my clients. That's it," Mack lied.

"So, what if she would have taken your offer of five grand?"

"I would have called my client. Nothing more."

"I'm sorry. I didn't mean anything by that 'pimp' comment. Anything I can do?"

"Not at this point, but I appreciate the offer." Mack picked up the hotel phone and called Bruno

"How's my girl?" Bruno asked.

"Cost me a lot of money," Mack said angrily.

"What happened?"

"She left my client very unhappy. Need I say more?"

"No. I'll get someone right over. Tell your client this one will be on the house."

"Don't bother," Mack said acting very angry. "We have one of his favorites on the way."

"It won't happen again," Bruno remarked. "I'll make sure of it."

"We'll be in touch," Mack said and then hung up the phone. He knew that he had put Alexis in a bad position, but he didn't feel sorry for her. She had become an unwitting player in this mission.

Bruno slammed the phone down. He was angry. He had warned her that she better cooperate. Alexis had made a fool of him. No one makes a fool of Bruno.

"Where is she?" Bruno yelled at one of his security detail.

"I saw her enter the club. She is getting ready to go on stage."

"Bring her to my office now," Bruno bellowed.

Bruno took a seat behind his large, cherry desk. He tried to calm himself before Alexis arrived. It was difficult. Bruno was a proud, but arrogant man. He had very little respect for women, especially his dancers or prostitutes. He saw women as an end to a means. He used them to get what he wanted. The door then opened and Alexis entered the office with one of Bruno's security detail.

"Wait outside," Bruno said to the man. The man left the room and closed the door behind him.

"Sit," Bruno said motioned at two chairs in front of his desk. Alexis took a seat in front of the desk. She knew that Bruno was not happy with her.

"What happened? The client was extremely unhappy."

"He wanted sex. I told you that I'm not doing that."

"You hypocrite!" screamed Bruno. "You were more than willing when you asked me for a job. You act like you never sold yourself before."

"I'm done with selling myself. I don't care if you like it or not. You mess with me and you'll deal with my boyfriend."

Bruno burst into laughter. "That little piece of crap?" Bruno rose from his chair and walked around to the front of the desk. "He ain't got the stones."

"He's got bigger stones than you," Alexis said with a smirk.

Bruno raised his right hand and backhanded Alexis across her face. The blow contained enough force to knock her out of her chair and onto the floor. Alexis got up off the floor with a very surprised look on her face. She wiped a small amount of blood from the corner of her mouth.

"You'll pay for this," Alexis screamed at Bruno.

"You cross me again and you won't be so lucky. Now, get back on stage or get out of my club."

Alexis stared at Bruno with a look that could kill. She pushed past Bruno and left the office. Alexis made up her mind. Bruno was not going to get away with this. She considered going to the authorities but she would have to implicate herself in Bruno's prostitution ring. Turning Bruno into the authorities would be a very risky and dangerous proposition. Bruno had many connections in the mob underworld. He also was rumored to have connections in law enforcement. Alexis decided not to leave the club just yet. If she left, she would not be able to get close to Bruno again, at least not without some groveling. She wanted him dead. She wasn't willing to do it herself, lest spending the rest of her life behind bars. She was willing however, to use others to achieve her goal.

Alexis changed into her dance outfit which was little more than a red thong bikini and a pair of red high-heeled shoes. She covered the bruise on her face with makeup and walked toward the stage. As she neared the stage, she saw her boyfriend standing against the back wall. She walked over to him and whispered in his ear.

"I've got to talk to you. Meet me outside the club after I get off the stage."

Alexis' boyfriend noticed the bruise on her cheek. His fist clenched tightly.

"Who did this to you?"

"I'll explain later. For now, don't do or say anything. Just meet me after I get off the stage."

Reluctantly, he agreed. Alexis then took the stage, noticing that Bruno was watching her. She acted like nothing happened, even giving Bruno a big smile. Bruno appeared satisfied that he made his point. Alexis finished her dancing, put on a beige raincoat to cover herself, and walked outside the club. Her boyfriend Michael was already waiting by his car in the parking lot. Alexis told him what had happened in Bruno's office. When he didn't react the way Alexis had expected, she decided to use a technique that she was a master at. Manipulation.

"I love you. I'm going to tell you something that I've never told anyone. Bruno raped me." Alexis was lying through her teeth. Bruno had never raped her. It was quite the opposite. She was more than willing to sleep with Bruno to get what she wanted.

"He raped you? When?"

"When I first started here. He told me that if I told anyone, he would kill me."

"Why didn't you tell me before?"

"I couldn't tell anyone," Alexis said continuing the lie. "I didn't want anyone to know that I had been raped."

"That piece of crap. We need to call the police."

"No. They won't believe me. He has friends in law enforcement." Seeing that the lies and deception were having the intended effect, she made up more lies. "He tried again tonight. I was able to fight him off."

"Why did you stay? We can leave now…let's go."

"He told me that if I left, he would have me killed. I'm scared. If only I can be rid of him, we can be together permanently."

"Let's just go home. He ain't worth it."

"You go home. I don't want to ever see you again. I thought you loved me." Alexis turned to walk back to the club.

"Wait. Just wait…I'll think of something."

Alexis ignored him and walked back into the club. He followed, begging her to stop. She didn't. Alexis then asked to see Bruno. One of the bouncers went to Bruno's office and returned a few minutes later. He told Alexis that she could go in. Bruno was waiting for her behind his desk.

"What do you want?" Bruno said without looking at Alexis.

"I'm ready to cooperate. Whatever you want me to do."

"Prove it," Bruno said leaning back in his chair.

Alexis took off her raincoat and slipped out of her bikini. She began to dance on the couch in Bruno's office. Bruno watched as Alexis worked her magic. She motioned for Bruno to join her on the couch and he readily complied. Alexis laid back on the couch and Bruno got on top of her.

As Bruno was attempting to remove his trousers, Alexis' boyfriend burst into the room. As soon as Alexis saw that her boyfriend entered the room, she started saying "Stop…Don't…Stop." She mouthed the words "Help Me!" to her boyfriend. Believing that Alexis was being raped, he ran across the room and pulled Bruno off of her.

Bruno had not seen him enter the room. He was shocked and surprised by what had just happened. One of Bruno's security guards heard the commotion and came into the office. Bruno had already started fighting with the boyfriend, pinning him to the ground and pummeling his face and chest. The security guard pulled Bruno off the man, ending the fight.

"Get him the hell out of here!" Bruno yelled.

The security guard grabbed the man by the neck and yanked him to his feet. The guard put him in a headlock, twisting his arm behind his back. The guard pushed the man through the office door leading to the parking lot. He threw him to the ground and proceeded to kick him repeatedly. The guard left him lay on the ground and walked back into the club. Alexis found Michael lying on the ground and rushed over to him. He was injured, but not seriously. Alexis helped him to his feet.

"You were right. I'm sorry that I didn't believe you."

"You okay? I love you so much. Thanks for saving me."

"I'm fine, but he's not getting away with this. I'm calling the police."

"No! If you do, he will kill you. Then he will kill me."

"What am I supposed to do?"

"Handle it yourself. Vinny said you ain't got the stones."

"I don't know…I still think that we should call the police."

"I'm done with you," Alexis said shoving Michael. "You catch him raping me and you want someone else to take care of it? I'll take care of it myself. Maybe Vinny was right, you ain't got the stones."

Alexis walked back into the club. Minutes later, Alexis saw Michael come back inside. She distracted the security guard so he wouldn't see him come in. The club was full of patrons, standing room only. Alexis made her way through the crowd and approached him.

"What are you doing here? You need to leave."

"I'm not leaving until I deal with Vinny."

"He beat you up last time. He'll just do the same thing again except much worse."

"Not this time. I need to get to his office."

"I'll distract the guard, but if you get caught…" Alexis stopped mid-sentence.

She saw the look on her boyfriend's face. She had never seen him this way before.

"Just do it."

Alexis distracted the guard near the entrance to Bruno's office by telling him that one of the patrons had touched her inappropriately. The guard immediately escorted the patron out of the club despite his denials. As soon as the guard had left his position, Alexis' boyfriend entered Bruno's office. The next thing that Alexis heard was the sound of gunfire. People froze and then, once the sound registered, they started to panic, running for the exits. Three security guards rushed to Bruno's office followed by Alexis.

Bruno laid in the center of his office, face down. The security guards rolled him over and were attempting to find a pulse. Bruno had been shot numerous times. A smile came across Alexis' face. Her plan had worked. Alexis walked out of the office as the paramedics were arriving. She left the club satisfied that she was able to manipulate Michael into killing Bruno.

Mack and Candy spent the night in the luxury hotel in Baltimore. Mack was awakened by the ringing of a cell phone. Mack answered it.

"Yeah, what's up?"

"The mission is complete. I don't know how you were able to

pull it off, but nonetheless, it is done."

"What are you talking about?"

"You don't know?" Rippy asked. "Turn on the television. It is all over the news."

Mack hung up the phone and turned on the bedroom television. Mack flipped through the channels until he came across the news. "*Strip Club Owner Killed in Love Triangle*" flashed across the screen. Mack turned up the volume and Candy sat up in the bed to watch the story. The on-site reporter was giving the details of the shooting.

"Vinny Bruno, the owner of The Shoe Store gentlemen's club was gunned down last night by a man believed to be the boyfriend of one of the dancers. The assailant had been identified as Michael Greene, a twenty-eight year old male from Baltimore. The murder was captured on surveillance video located inside of Bruno's office. Sources close to the investigation state that Bruno was engaged in a love triangle with one of the dancers and the alleged assailant. Police are searching for Greene and an arrest is imminent."

Mack turned to Candy and told her that it would be best if they left the hotel as soon as possible. Candy started getting dressed. Mack slipped on his clothes and waited for Candy to finish getting ready. They checked out of the room and headed back to Candy's hotel in Frederick. On the drive back to the hotel, Mack listened to a local radio station for updates on the shooting. As the approached Candy's hotel, the radio station provided the latest news on the incident. Police had spotted Greene's car and gave pursuit. Greene, traveling more than a hundred miles-per-hour in an attempt to elude police, lost control of his vehicle and crashed into an embankment. Greene, and a female passenger in the vehicle, were killed. The female riding in Greene's vehicle is believed to be Alexis Gibson, the woman allegedly involved in the love triangle.

Mack turned off the radio. The mission was now complete. He was glad that he didn't need to kill Bruno. There were three members left. Rippy would be the final target. He wouldn't be the one to kill the two unless it was absolutely necessary or to protect his life or Candy's. He would however, be more than happy to kill Rippy.

CHAPTER FIFTEEN

Mack and Candy pulled into their hotel. They went up to their room and Mack checked his motion sensor video camera. No one had been in the room since they left. Candy went to take a shower and Mack laid down on the couch to catch some shuteye. When he awoke, he noticed that he had a text message from Rippy. He picked up the phone and opened the message.

"Next mission documents are in the newspaper outside of your door."

Mack opened the room door and picked up the complimentary newspaper, which much thicker than normal. The brown envelope tucked inside the newspaper came as no surprise. Mack slipped it into his backpack and went to check on Candy. She was in the bedroom sound asleep. Mack went back in the living room, pulled the envelope, and ran a security check. Feeling confident that it was safe, Mack sliced the bottom of the envelope and removed the contents. *"Charles T. Stroud—Selected for Termination for Crimes Committed Against the United States."*

Stroud was an elderly gentleman. For a man in his early seventies, he appeared to be in good physical shape. His hair was like polished silver. He had piercing, light blue eyes which seemed to look right through you. His ears were larger than normal and accentuated the thinness of his face. Mack pulled out the dossier and began to read. Stroud was involved in human trafficking and smuggling. He ran a large organization that involved the sale of young women into the sex slave market. Stroud lured young women into the U.S. on the promise of citizenship and a better life. He arranged for immigration documents and kept the women in makeshift brothels where they were forced into a life of prostitution. Stroud confiscated the immigration documents and passports, keeping the young women from leaving the country and returning home. Stroud kept the women from going to the authorities by intimidation and physical violence. In a foreign country, often not able to speak the language, the women had little choice but to cooperate. Stroud was making large profits for the organization. The more money he made, the more he had to contribute to the central fund.

Stroud had been involved in harboring illegal aliens and charged with unlawful restraint of a group of young females. At his initial court appearance, the prosecution was forced to withdrawal the charges when the witnesses failed to appear. On his way out of the courtroom, he was approached by a man claiming to have arranged the dismissal of the court case. This man gave Stroud the option of joining his organization or charges would be re-filed and the prosecution would start again. In return, Stroud would receive protection from the authorities. Stroud was reluctant to accept the man's offer, but reconsidered at the thought of spending years behind bars. At his age, even a ten year prison term would be a life sentence.

The moment Stroud joined he organization, he lost operational control of his human trafficking enterprise. He needed approval for nearly everything. Stroud grew tired of the constant interference in his operations. He now earned only a fraction of the money before this chance encounter. He decided to leave the organization. Stroud asked for a face-to-face meeting. At first, the request was turned down, but after Stroud alluded to suspected investigations by the federal government, the meeting was approved. He provided Stroud the address of a residence outside of Frederick, Maryland.

Stroud drove to Frederick for his meeting. The entrance to the residence was protected by a black metal security fence. Stroud entered the four digit security code provided and the gates opened allowing him to drive into the property. After parking his car at the front of the house, he walked to the front door of the home. As he was about to knock on the door, the door opened and a large man dressed in a black military-style uniform let Stroud into the residence. He instructed Stroud to have a seat in the library and someone would be with him in a few moments.

The library was very large. Mahogany bookcases lined the wall and an oversized cherry desk sat in the center of the room. Stroud was extremely jealous. He knew that the majority of the proceeds from his criminal enterprise were being used to purchase residences like this one. He was doing all the work, taking all the risk, and someone else was reaping all the rewards. He made up his mind. He was going to tell the leader that he was through with this organization. He would take his chances with the authorities, turning state's evidence and hoping for a lenient sentence.

"You called this meeting. State your business," Rippy said.

"I'm done. I'm leaving the organization."

"Then you'll spend the rest of your life in prison," Rippy replied with no emotion.

"Doubtful. I have enough information to cut a deal with the authorities."

Rippy's demeanor changed. Stroud had threatened to turn on the organization, something that Rippy would not tolerate.

"I'm going to give you a choice. You can continue your current operations or you can die."

"Not much of a choice is it?" Stroud asked rhetorically. Stroud rose from his chair and started to walk out of the library. Before he could exit the room, Rippy asked "What do you choose?"

"I choose life," Stroud said as he left the room.

Stroud was not convinced that Rippy was serious. If he thought that his life was bad before the meeting with Rippy, it soon became far worse. Everywhere Stroud went, he was followed by one of Rippy's men. His phones were tapped and his mail was intercepted and read. Rippy placed some of his men in an undercover capacity, looking for any sign of betrayal. Stroud had awaken on numerous occasions only to find someone standing over his bed, pointing a pistol at him. Fear was now an everyday portion of Stroud's life.

As Mack read the dossier, he learned that Stroud had a horse ranch just south of Louisville, Kentucky. Mack decided that he would not need Candy's assistance in this mission. He had no idea yet on how he would terminate Stroud, but he would make it look like an accident if possible. Mack was disgusted by Stroud's activities. He thought about all the women who were being held against their will and force into prostitution. Human trafficking was increasing at a rapid pace. Mack now had a chance to make a significant impact on this horrible criminal enterprise. He put the dossier back into the brown envelope and returned it to his backpack. He would be leaving for Kentucky in a few hours.

Mack went into the bedroom and laid down in the bed next to Candy. He wanted to spend as much time as possible with her. Being with her made him feel good about himself. He was happy. Candy, realizing that Mack had entered the bed, turned towards him.

"You're leaving soon?"

"Yeah, I just got a new assignment," Mack whispered. "I am leaving in a few hours.

"Am I staying or going?"

"Staying."

Mack hated to tell her that she couldn't go with him. She had been a valuable asset to his mission. More importantly, he missed her deeply when he was away from her.

Candy's face showed the disappointment she was feeling. She wanted to go along, but didn't want to get in the way. She would do as Mack asked, but not without great reluctance.

"How long will you be gone?"

"Can't say. Hopefully, not for more than a week. If you leave this hotel, I want to know immediately."

After another great breakfast, Mack kissed Candy goodbye. She clung to him tightly. Candy's eyes welled with tears. Mack promised her that he would return as soon as possible. Mack's heart hung heavy as he walked to the parking lot and got in the 4x4 pickup truck that Rippy placed in the hotel parking lot.

Mack punched the address in the GPS and drove west on Interstate 70 on his way to Louisville. During the nine hour journey, Mack thought about his current mission. The surveillance photos indicated that Stroud's horse ranch consisted of a home and a large horse barn. The home sat at the end of a long paved driveway that wound its way past large sycamore trees that lined its path. A large section of heavily wooded land bordered the north edge of the ranch. Mack decided that he would use the concealment of the woods to conduct surveillance of Stroud.

Mack arrived in the area of Stroud's ranch just before nightfall. The sky was clear and the stars were beginning to emerge for their nightly performance. Mack did not have any problem finding the ranch. Two large, black metal columns supported a wrought iron sign with the words *Blackstone Ranch* spelled out in gold painted metal letters. Mack drove past the entrance and turned onto a small road which paralleled the heavily wooded section of Stroud's ranch.

Mack found a place to pull off where his vehicle would not be seen from the road. He retrieved a small pair of binoculars from his backpack and headed towards the ranch through the woods. The woods were very dark, but Mack's unique ability to see in the dark made it easy for him to navigate his way to the edge of the woods line. He stayed in the darkness and peered through the binoculars.

The house was dimly lit, a yellow light from window candles shining through white lace curtains. Mack scanned the rest of the house looking for any sign of life. He noticed the distinctive flicker of light from a television in a rear window. The only other illumination came from a bright light shining down on large doors on the horse barn. Mack scanned the rest of the grounds and spotted a farm tractor hooked to a hay wagon sitting beside the barn. Unable to see inside the house at this distance, he decided to get closer to the house for a better look. He crossed the grounds, keeping in the darkness, and made his way to the rear of the house. Mack stood motionless against the rear of the house waiting to see if his movement had been detected.

After waiting several moments, Mack knew that he had not been detected. He looked in the window and saw Shroud sitting in a brown leather chair watching horse racing on television. Although it would be easy for him to enter the house and terminate Stroud, his best course of action would be to return the next day and conduct additional surveillance. He didn't want to act until he was sure that he could complete the mission without being seen.

Mack retreated from the house and returned to the woods. He

retraced his path back to his vehicle and drove to the hotel arranged by Rippy. He wanted to return to the woods line before daybreak, concealing his movement under the cover of darkness. Mack undressed and laid down on the bed.

Early the next morning, Mack arose at the sound of the alarm. He had only been able to sleep a few hours. His mind was filled with finding an exit strategy. He needed to find a way for him, and more importantly for Candy, to disappear and be safe. Other than several thousand dollars given to him on previous missions, Mack had not been paid the five hundred thousand dollars per target promised by Rippy. Mack decided that he would press Rippy for three million dollars, half of the total amount. If Rippy balked at paying the amount, Mack would cease the mission. Mack was sure that Rippy had no intention of paying him at the conclusion of the mission. He would get as much as he could from Rippy now.

Mack got dressed and put his .22 caliber pistol and silencer in his jacket pocket. He wore camouflage clothes to blend in with the locals, Kentucky being the hunter's paradise that it is. Mack jumped in his truck and drove back to the same spot he found the previous evening. He got out of the truck and walked into the woods.

The sun was just beginning to rise, melting away the thin layer of fog that covered the ground like a white linen blanket. Mack made his way through the woods towards the ranch house. Once he arrived at the edge of the woods, he pulled out his binoculars and scanned the area. He didn't notice anything different about the ranch this early morning. The tractor and wagon were still parked by the barn. He would use the hay wagon as cover to conduct more surveillance. He needed to leave the woods and cross the open field towards the barn. He would not have the cover of darkness to conceal his movements this time. He would have to use stealth. By keeping low, he would use the farm tractor and wagon to block the view from the house of his movement.

Mack moved slowly and with purpose. He knew that if he could not see the rear of the house during his movement, it was not likely that he could be seen by anyone looking outside the windows. Mack made it to the hay wagon without being detected. He climbed up the stake body wagon and lowered himself carefully down the other side. Once inside, he covered himself with loose hay. Looking through the slats in the side of the wagon, he had a good view of the rear of the house and the entrance to the horse barn. He considered shooting Stroud from this position, but preferred making it look like an accident if at all possible. He wanted to see how things developed before resorting to his pistol.

Mack knew that he may have to wait for hours until Stroud appeared. Surveillance was ninety-five percent boredom and five percent adrenalin. More than an hour passed until Mack saw some movement in the house. A small figure walked past one of the windows, probably a woman. Then Mack heard shouting. He couldn't make out the words being said, but he could tell that it was a woman's voice. He heard sounds of breaking glass and the scream of a woman's voice. The rear door of the house opened and a young woman came through the door crashing to the ground.

Stroud appeared and walked over to the young girl, yanking her to her feet by her hair. The woman started screaming from the pain, trying to break Stroud's grip from her hair. Mack had to make a conscious effort to restrain himself. Stroud pushed the girl back into the house and warned her that if she attempted to leave, he would hunt her down and kill her. Stroud then walked toward the tractor and hay wagon. He picked up a pitch fork and threw it in the back of the wagon. The pitch fork landed within inches of Mack.

Stroud jumped on the tractor and started the engine. As the tractor started to move, Mack considered jumping from the hay wagon, but decided to remain concealed. Stroud drove the tractor away from the barn and headed towards a group of horses standing in a field that bordered the woods. The field was located at the bottom of a steep hill.

As the tractor started the steep descent, Mack felt the hay wagon start to slide. Stroud was descending the slope at too fast of a pace. He was angry with the young woman and this anger was affecting his reasoning and judgment. Realizing that he was traveling too fast down the hill, Stroud panicked and slammed on the brakes. It was too late. The sudden braking, coupled with the wet ground, caused the tractor to slide sideways. The abrupt movement whipped the hay wagon counterclockwise. The top heavy wagon slid a short distance before the wheels caught causing the entire wagon to flip over. Mack was thrown violently from one side of the wagon to the other. He impacted the side of the wagon nearly knocking him unconscious. Mack felt himself starting to blackout. He focused his mind to remain conscious.

The next thing Mack heard was a large crashing sound and the tractor engine start to sputter. Within a few seconds, the engine stopped. Mack was covered completely with hay and in entire darkness. He laid still for a moment, trying to determine the extent of his injuries. He felt a sharp pain in his shoulder and his left arm was numb. He tried to push himself upright, but his left arm betrayed him causing him to fall back onto his stomach. Mack rolled onto his back and sat upright. The wagon had landed on its left side spilling most of its contents.

Ignoring the pain in his left shoulder, Mack pulled himself up and looked through the front slats of the wagon and saw that the tractor had also flipped over onto its left side. He did not see Stroud in the driver's seat. Although the tractor was equipped with a seat belt, Stroud did not fasten it before driving away from the barn.

Mack pulled himself out of the wagon, his shoulder causing him immense pain. His left arm hung useless by his side. He still could not see Stroud. Mack then heard a moaning sound. He walked around to the other side of the tractor and found Stroud pinned underneath. The tractor had landed on top of Stroud, crushing his lower extremities. Although conscious, Stroud was seriously injured. Mack knew that he couldn't remove the immense weight of the tractor from Stroud's body.

Stroud saw that someone was present and asked for help. "Please help me."

"I'll go for help, but you had better make peace with your maker."

The gravity of the situation appeared to have a dramatic effect on Stroud.

"My legs are cold and it's getting harder to breathe. Please call for help now."

"I don't think help will arrive in time," Mack said honestly.

"Take this gold ring off my finger...please...I don't want to die with it on. Do whatever you want with it. It has ruined my life."

Mack removed the ring from Stroud's left hand and placed it in his pocket. Mack noticed the familiar insignia.

"Looks like a very nice ring. Why would you not want to die with it on?"

"It is a symbol of death. It represents a secret society. One I regretted joining. The biggest mistake of my life."

"What organization? What are you talking about?" Mack asked.

"I can't tell you. Your life would be in great danger."

"Then take your secret to the grave. May God have mercy on your soul," Mack said as he started to walk away.

"Wait. Don't go. I'll tell you, but please get help first."

"Okay. I'll call for help," Mack said acting like he was calling 911.

"Who is the leader of this organization?"

"I don't know his full name. All I know is that the person calls himself Rippy."

"Where does this guy live?"

"Maryland. I met him there on several occasions."

Stroud gave Mack the street address and also the combination to the safe inside Stroud's house.

"Here's the combination to a safe inside my house. You will find documents that will help the authorities to prosecute him. If I don't make it, at least I will have the last laugh on Rippy."

"No. I will have the last laugh," Mack said as he placed the ring back on Stroud's finger as Stroud took his last breath and died.

Mack walked back to the tree line and made his way through the woods to his vehicle. His left arm was still mostly numb causing him to use his right hand to move it. Once at his hotel, Mack carefully removed his jacket and shirt. He noticed that his left shoulder was pushed out of place. The fall in the hay wagon had dislocated his left shoulder. Placing his shoulder against the door frame of the bathroom, he pushed against the wall. He twisted his body in a clockwise motion forcing pressure against his shoulder. The quick twist forced his shoulder back into the proper position. Mack then felt a sharp pain down his left arm and then the numbness was gone.

Mack packed his belongings and checked out of the hotel. He wanted to leave the area and head back towards Frederick as soon as possible. The mission had been completed much sooner than even he expected. Ten of the twelve targets had been eliminated. That meant the next target would be the last before Mack would set his sights on Rippy. With only one target remaining, Mack knew that Rippy would soon make his move.

Mack decided that he would not phone Rippy to inform him that the mission was complete yet. He knew that Rippy had probably been conducting surveillance of Stroud and he would know soon enough that Stroud was dead. Mack threw his gear in the truck and started on the nine hour journey back to Maryland. A few hours out of Louisville, Mack received a phone call from Rippy.

"Well done, Mack," Rippy said when Mack answered the phone.

"Not my doing, but it is complete nonetheless."

"Makes no difference. The target has been eliminated," Rippy said in his usual solemn tone.

"We need to talk about payment," Mack said.

"Payment will be made when all twelve targets are complete."

"I want half now."

"That was not the deal," Rippy replied. "You will receive payment upon mission completion."

"There was no mention of payment terms other than the amount," Mack spouted back. "I've kept my end of the bargain. If you want me to continue, I want half now."

"I'll see what I can do. I might be able to transfer funds to an account in your name."

"No accounts," snapped Mack. "Three million in cash."

"Cash?" exclaimed Rippy. "Where am I supposed to come up with three million in cash?"

"I'm sure you're very resourceful. The government has plenty of cash."

Rippy reluctantly agreed.

"Okay, but it will take some time. The final payment however, will be deposited into an account."

"Fine. I'll start the next mission upon receipt of the cash," Mack said as he hung up the phone. Mack knew that Rippy was not happy. He didn't care. He needed the money to disappear and start a new life with Candy. Besides, Rippy would not need the money where he was going. *You can't take it with you.* Mack laughed to himself.

CHAPTER SIXTEEN

Mack arrived in Frederick, Maryland late in the afternoon. He was exhausted and his shoulder ached from the earlier accident at Stroud's ranch. He was growing tired of the whole mission. He wanted to finish the job and put it all behind him. He regretted getting involved with Rippy. The only part he didn't regret was his involvement with Candy.

Mack pulled into Candy's hotel and took a quick look around the parking lot. He spotted one of Rippy's Raiders sitting in a vehicle at the far end of the parking lot. Mack thought about driving past and waiving at the man, but thought it was best to not let on that he knew he was being watched.

Mack pulled into a parking spot which had a view of Candy's room. The curtains were pulled shut and he couldn't tell if the room was occupied. He hoped that she was there. Mack made his way to her room and knocked on the door. There was no response. Mack left his keys to the room with Candy before he departed for Louisville. Mack retrieved his smart phone and pulled up the images of the video surveillance cameras in the room. Switching between views, Mack was able to determine that no one was inside the room, but it appeared as though Candy was still living there. Her clothes were lying on the bed and her shoes were near the couch. Mack sent Candy a text message asking her how she was doing. Within a minute, Mack got a return text message saying that Candy was taking a dip in the hotel pool.

Mack went down to the pool and saw Candy sitting at the edge with her feet in the water. The sight of Candy in her white bikini brought a smile to his face. Mack walked through the door and approached Candy from behind.

"Miss me?" asked Mack.

Candy spun around and jumped to her feet when she saw Mack.

"Paul! I missed you so much," Candy said embracing Mack tightly.

Mack could feel her wet bathing suit against his body. He didn't care one bit. He was together with his soul mate.

"When did you get in?"

"Just a couple of minutes ago. I can use a beer."

"Me too. I've got plenty of cold ones just waiting for you to return."

Candy slipped on a pair of sweat pants and one of Mack's t-shirts. Mack smiled at the sight of Candy wearing his clothes. He had to admit, she looked a whole lot better in it then he did. They walked to their room arm in arm. On the way back, Mack whispered in Candy's ear. "I've got something to tell you."

Candy whispered back, "Me too."

Mack couldn't wait to hear what Candy had to say. Once back at the room, Mack asked Candy to get dressed for dinner. He wanted to find a quiet place without the prying ears of Rippy. Mack and Candy left the hotel and found a steakhouse restaurant.

"You told me a while ago that you weren't being honest with me," Mack said.

"I tried to tell you, but you stopped me."

"I'm ready to listen now," Mack said impatiently. He needed to be absolutely sure that he could trust Candy before embarking on the final two missions.

"Our first meeting was not a chance encounter," Candy said sheepishly.

"Why not?" Mack asked.

"Because I was instructed to make contact with you."

"By whom?"

"The government. I was told to develop a relationship with you and inform my superiors on your whereabouts and activities."

"You're an agent of the U.S. Government?"

"Obviously, not a very good one. I just blew my cover."

"Why are you telling me this?"

"Because I don't want to do this anymore. I know that if I do, bad things will happen to you and I can't let that happen," Candy said as she started to cry.

"They could put you in jail for this. You know that right?"

"Yes, but I don't care anymore. I wasn't even sure that I could do it after seeing you for the first time. There was something about you that I couldn't explain. Something good and honest about you. Not like the things that I was told."

"Things like what?

"Truthfully, not much. At least not much detail. I was told to develop a relationship with you and help gather evidence of wrong doing. They told me that you were a very bad person, but I knew in my heart that you couldn't be."

"So you seduced me to gain evidence and information?" Mack asked holding back a smile.

"I wasn't required to sleep with you. Had it been anyone else, I never would have. But I felt an instant connection with you. I'm sorry. So very sorry."

"You've done this before? Seduced men for your own gain?"

"No. This is my first, and my last mission."

"Well, I'm glad that you are being honest with me now. I know that beyond a doubt."

"How do you know?"

"Never mind how I know. But now that you've told me who you really are, your life is in danger."

"Danger? They told me that it could be a bit risky, but that I would never be in any real danger."

"Who told you that?"

"Rippy."

"Who is Rippy?" Mack said continuing the ruse.

"He is my superior. He is the one that gave me the orders to follow. He is the one that I provided all the information about you to."

"What were Rippy's latest instructions?"

"Several hours before you got here, Rippy called me. He told me that the mission is over and that I needed to end the relationship with you. He said that after I told you that I wasn't interested in you anymore, I would move on to an entirely new mission."

"What else did he tell you?"

"That I had performed exemplary during the mission and wanted to recruit me for more intensive covert operations which may involve having to eliminate a target. I told him that I didn't know if I could kill someone. He said that I would have no choice. If I didn't comply with his orders, he would have me prosecuted for treason."

Mack couldn't help but let out a small smile.

"You think that's funny?" Candy said choking back the tears.

"No. Just unrealistic. You won't get prosecuted for treason. Breaking the beauty barrier perhaps, but not treason," Mack said with another smile.

"You really aren't the bad person they say you are?"

"Did you see me break any laws?"

"No. I can't believe I get myself into these situations. I also manage to mess things up."

"Do you trust me?" Mack asked as he wiped the tears from Candy's cheeks.

"Yes. My mind wonders who you are, but my heart knows that you are a good person."

"Then do as Rippy tells you." Candy's eyes began to swell with tears.

"No. I won't end my relationship with you. I love you."

"I didn't say anything about ending it, just pretend you did. Don't tell Rippy what you told me. I might be able to get you out of this situation."

"But what about you?"

"Just trust me right now. You trusted me enough to tell me who you really are, so I need blind trust from you. Nothing short of it. If I tell you to do something, you do it without questions. Understand?"

"Okay."

"And one other thing. You must act like nothing has happened. No more talk about what you told me."

"But…" Mack cut her off mid-sentence. "I told you, do as I say without question."

Several days passed without any contact with Rippy. Mack enjoyed the time he was spending with Candy, but was anxious to finish the mission. He was wondering when the next information would arrive when he heard a knock at the door. Mack opened the door and was greeted by a member of the hotel staff. He handed Mack a brown envelope and a large black duffle bag.

Mack took the items into the room and opened the black bag. The bag was filled with stacks of hundred-dollar bills. Mack had never seen so much money in his life. Suspicious of Rippy, Mack first counted the money. Three million dollars. Next, he used his smart phone to determine if any of Rippy's black disc tracking devices were located in the bag. Mack found several discs sewn into the bag. He did a quick scan on the money, but didn't find any tracking devices. Mack now had the funds he needed for Candy to disappear until the mission was completed. He grabbed the brown envelope and sliced open the bottom. He pulled out the dossier and photographs. As with each mission before, he read the top cover sheet.

Morgan Dillinger—Selected for Termination for Crimes Against the United States.

Mack removed the photographs and flipped through them. Dillinger was in his late forties, nearly six feet tall with a muscular build. He had dark brown hair and green eyes. As Mack carefully studied the photographs, he stumbled upon one major finding. In all the photographs, Dillinger was not wearing any rings. The other thing that struck Mack as odd was Dillinger's age. He was much younger than all the other targets. If he was right, he needed to get Candy in a safe place until Rippy had been eliminated.

Mack found Candy in the bedroom and told her that the time had come for him to leave. Candy had a friend in Philadelphia. She could stay with her for a period of time and arranged to meet her at a large shopping mall outside of Philadelphia. The large crowds and the massive parking areas made it an ideal location for Candy to disappear from Rippy's ever prying eyes. Candy would only need to disappear for a few days at most.

As Mack instructed, Candy packed all of the items given to her by Rippy in a separate suitcase. Once Candy was packed, Mack did a scan of Candy's personal effects for the small tracking devices. Mack received numerous signals only from the suitcase containing the items provided by Rippy. He then scanned the rest of Candy's belongings and didn't locate any other tracking devices. Mack gave Candy a prepaid cell phone for her to use. Candy then packed her car and drove out of the hotel parking lot towards Philadelphia.

Mack jumped in his truck and drove towards Baltimore. The dossier indicated that Dillinger lived in the outskirts of Baltimore. This was the same area during the mission to terminate Bruno. Rippy did not provide any satellite photographs of Dillinger's location. All Mack had was an address.

On his way to Baltimore, Mack stopped at numerous locations. He wanted to throw Rippy off the trail, deceiving Rippy into believing that he had dropped Candy off at one of these locations. At one particular location, Mack buried the large black duffle bag. As Mack neared Baltimore, he received a phone call from Candy on the prepaid cell phone he purchased.

"All went as planned," Candy said.

"Great news," Mack replied. "Remember to use only the cash that I provided. Any use of credit cards will alert Rippy as to your location."

"Please be safe, Paul."

Now that Candy was safe, he could turn his focus on Dillinger. There was no longer a need to make it look like an accident. Dillinger was going to try and kill him. It was now a matter of kill or be killed.

It didn't take long for Mack to find Dillinger's address. He waited until nightfall before driving to the area. Darkness would provide concealment and help him get close to residence undetected. Mack parked the truck several blocks from the house.

He grabbed the cell phone Rippy provided, a small night vision camera, and the pair of shoes that contained the tracking devices. He put the .22 caliber pistol with silencer in his jacket pocket and started towards the house. Weaving his way through the alley, Mack watched carefully to see if he was being followed.

In between one of the alleys, Mack encountered a homeless person.

"Can you help a brother out?"

"It depends. I'm not giving you a handout, but if you're willing to work for it," Mack said holding out a crisp hundred-dollar bill.

"Who do I have to kill?" asked the man.

"Nobody. I only want you to deliver this cell phone to a house."

"That's it? A hundred dollars for delivering a cell phone? What's the catch?"

"No catch. I'm not risking my life in this neighborhood."

"Sounds like you afraid. Gotta be worth more than a hundred bucks to you then."

"I can give you something else to sweeten the deal," Mack said as he pulled out the pair of shoes with the tracking devices from his bag.

"Man, those some nice shoes," the man said snatching the shoes from Mack's grasp. "You've got a deal."

Mack handed the man the cell phone and the money.

"There's an extra hundred dollars in it if you can do it without being seen."

The man jumped to his feet, grabbed the other hundred dollars and started towards Dillinger's residence.

Mack followed the man at a distance. The homeless man kept

in the shadows and snuck his way towards the house. Mack was impressed with the man's ability to move without being seen. Living on the streets sure makes one very familiar with their surroundings.

Dillinger sat across the street in a dark colored cargo van. He was tracking movement on a small LCD display device. Photographs of Mack were taped to dash of the vehicle. Dillinger's plan was to allow Mack to enter the residence and then strike when he exited the house. Dillinger was not a government trained assassin, but he had killed numerous people before on Rippy's orders. Dillinger carefully watched the display as the target approached the residence. He could now see someone moving in the dark. The figure moved to the rear of the house and disappeared into the darkness. Dillinger grabbed his pistol and started to exit the vehicle. As he opened the door and put his foot on the ground, he felt a sharp pain on the side of his head before he blacked out.

Dillinger awoke and found himself hog-tied in the back of the cargo van, lying face down. When Mack saw that Dillinger had regained consciousness, he placed one of his boots on the side of Dillinger's head and started to apply pressure. Dillinger tried to speak but had a rag stuffed in his mouth. Mack removed the rag.

"Stop!" Dillinger screamed.

"Quiet," Mack said releasing pressure from the side of Dillinger's face. "Who sent you?"

"Nobody."

"Nobody, huh?" Mack shoved the picture of himself in front of Dillinger's face. "Then why do you have a picture of me?"

"Don't know what you are talking about. Now let me go."

"I'll give you one more chance. Tell me the truth and you

might live," Mack said putting greater pressure with his foot on Dillinger's face.

"Go screw yourself," Dillinger replied.

Mack stuffed the rag back into Dillinger's mouth. He had given him an opportunity to tell the truth, but chose to play ignorant. Mack pulled out the dossier and began to read. Dillinger was directed to terminate an individual by the name of Paul Brittan. Mack thought it was odd that Rippy still used his covert name. Upon completion, Dillinger was to text the word "Done" to a telephone number listed in the dossier. Mack recognized the telephone number. It was Rippy's. Mack typed the word "Done" into Dillinger's cell phone and sent the message. Within minutes, Rippy sent a reply text message. *"Well done. Standby for next mission."* In addition to the photographs of Mack, Dillinger had some of Candy. On one of the photos, Candy's face was circled with "make it hurt" written below.

"Who is this girl?" Mack screamed at the man.

"Don't know."

Mack placed his foot on the man's neck and began to cut off the air supply.

"OK…OK…She's the next target."

"Explain," Mack said.

"I've been instructed to eliminate her after the guy in the photographs."

"Who sent you here?"

"Rippy. I don't know his first name. All I know is that he calls himself Rippy."

"Where does he live?"

"I don't know. I've only been there one time. I can't remember the address."

"Describe it. What city?"

Dillinger gave the exact same description of the house as Stroud provided. Mack was certain that this was Rippy's residence.

"Where's the girl?" Mack asked.

"Don't know. Rippy said he would give me the address once he located her. He said she disappeared."

"Who wrote the words on her photograph?"

"I guess Rippy did. He told me to make her suffer. He said she betrayed him. He was very upset. Now let me go."

"How much did he pay you?"

"Ten thousand per target."

"What else did Rippy tell you?"

"Nothing. Only that I was to bring him a pink crystal amulet from around your neck. I needed it for proof of your death. I wouldn't get paid without it. He said it belonged to him."

Mack felt the rage building inside him.

"How much is it worth for me not to kill you?" Mack asked.

"Whatever you want. Did Rippy send you?"

Mack decided to play along.

"Yeah, Rippy sent me. He told me where you were located. He used the other guy as bait. You fell right into his trap. Any last words?"

"Let me go and I'll disappear. I'll pay you double whatever Rippy is paying you."

"Tempting offer. How do I know that you won't call Rippy the second I let you go? I don't want Rippy after me."

"I give you my word. I don't have much else in life. I have never gone back on my word. If Rippy is after me, I'd kill him myself if I could."

"You're going to get your chance," Mack said.

Mack scanned Dillinger's vehicle for any tracking devices. Surprised that the vehicle did not contain any, he scanned Dillinger's body and got the same result. Mack grabbed Dillinger's cell phone and switched it off. He then removed the battery. Mack left Dillinger in the back of the van and jumped in the driver's seat and drove off.

Mack located Rippy's residence and parked several blocks away. The front entrance was protected by a large gate as described by Stroud. Mack untied Dillinger and confirmed his desire to eliminate Rippy. Dillinger was even more ready to do the job after riding hog-tied in the back of his own van. Mack returned Dillinger's weapon unloaded. He gave him the bullets separately.

"Here's your gun. You can load it on the way to Rippy's. I'll be watching every move you make. At the first sign of betrayal, you will die. Terminate the target and you disappear. Understand?"

"I gave you my word," Dillinger replied. "I'll kill Rippy or die trying."

Dillinger left the vehicle and started walking towards the house with Mack following at a short distance. A thick hedgerow surrounded the property on three sides. Dillinger slipped between the bushes and disappeared from sight. Mack followed Dillinger through the hedgerows, careful as he exited the thick bushes. Once through, Mack saw Dillinger approaching the rear of the residence. A large veranda sat at the rear of the residence covering a large set of white French doors. Dillinger was crouched down, prying the doors with a small knife. He opened the door and slipped inside.

Mack slipped inside the house behind Dillinger. He lost sight of him but could hear the sound of his footsteps. Mack moved in sync with the footsteps, screening his movement. As he turned the corner, he saw Dillinger slowly turning a door knob and pushing the door slightly open. Dillinger then entered the room. Mack quickly made his way to the doorway, staying unseen, but able to eavesdrop into the room. Mack heard a distinctive voice. It was Rippy.

"What are you doing here?" Rippy asked.

"Settling the score. You should have never crossed me," Dillinger replied.

"What are you talking about?"

"You set me up!"

Mack peered into the room and saw Dillinger standing in front of the desk, pointing his pistol at Rippy.

"It wasn't I who set you up," Rippy said. "I believe I know who did. Now, put that weapon down."

Dillinger started to lower his weapon. As he did so, Rippy pulled out a .45 caliber pistol from under his desk and fired one round at Dillinger striking him in the chest. Dillinger fell to the ground from the fatal shot.

Rippy placed the pistol on top of his desk and picked up the phone. Before he could dial any number, Mack entered the room.

"Put the phone down."

Rippy placed the receiver back on the phone and looked at his pistol sitting on his desk.

"Don't even think about it," Mack commanded.

Keeping his pistol drawn on Rippy, Mack picked up Dillinger's weapon with his gloved hand.

"I thought you were dead," Rippy said. "I haven't given you enough credit. What tipped you off?"

"The rings," Mack replied. "All of the targets wore a distinctive ring. Like the one you are wearing."

Rippy looked down at the gold ring he was wearing with the distinctive design.

"Understood," Rippy said in his usual solemn tone. "I hadn't even considered that the rings would be my downfall. What else did you learn?"

"You are the leader of the Ring of Twelve".

"Ring of Twelve…Ring of Twelve," Rippy said to himself. "I like that name. I guess I can't convince you to join this Ring of Twelve".

"Not a chance," Mack replied.

"Then your girlfriend dies," Rippy said as a smile came across his face.

"She pretty safe," Mack said.

"I wouldn't assume what you don't know as fact," Rippy said with a smirk.

"You're bluffing," Mack said placing the gun against Rippy's temple.

"I'm surprised at you, Mack. You got emotionally involved. The downfall of every assassin. I guess the only way to prove it is for you to hear her voice."

Rippy reached for the phone lying near the pistol on his desk.

"Touch that pistol, you die."

Rippy picked up the phone, put it on speaker, and dialed a number.

"Go ahead, I'm listening," Becker said.

"Put the bitch on the phone," Rippy said angrily.

"Hello? Hello? Why are you doing this to me?" Candy's voice crackled across the speaker.

Mack recognized the number displayed on the cell phone. The same number used by the thugs that broke into his house. Rippy hung up the phone.

"Believe me now?" Rippy asked.

"Yeah, so what? Go ahead and kill her. She is just as involved in this organization as you are."

"You are wrong, Mack. Dead wrong. She truly believed that she was working for the government. So far, you've killed people who deserved to be killed. You want her death on your conscious?"

"Mack put the pistol against Rippy's head again.

"What? Are you going to kill me?"

"Perhaps," Mack said mocking Rippy.

Mack started to squeeze the trigger when the phone rang.

"Answer it. Put it on speaker."

Rippy answered the phone. "What is it?"

"We've got a problem. We found where the black bag was buried. We dug it up and when we opened it, it exploded."

"What happened to the money?"

"All burned up. We found a few hundred-dollar bills, but that was it."

"Unfortunate. Forget about it," Rippy said as he hung up the phone.

"Now, you have nothing."

"Don't matter. It was dirty money anyway," Mack lied. Mack had only planted a small amount of the money with the explosives in the black bag.

"I guess we're even now," Rippy said.

"How did you learn about *Operation Jungle Fever*?"

"Well, like you, I did operational time. I was a government assassin trained in the same manner. Before I left the government's employ, I came across a classified file on *Operation Jungle Fever*. I knew that one day that information would come in handy."

"You sold your soul for money," Mack said.

"There is nothing else in life except for money," Rippy spouted. "Besides, you just did the same thing."

"Not the same," Mack said angrily. "I did it for my country."

"That's a joke." Rippy said laughing out loud. "What about the three million?"

"Wouldn't have been necessary if you had been whom you said you were. Makes no difference now. It is what it is."

"So we're even then?"

"Not a chance. Why did you want the pink crystal amulet? Dillinger said it belonged to you."

"It did at one time. I gave it to your mother."

"You gave it to her? You knew my mother?"

"Yes, Johnny. That is what she used to call you isn't it?"

"Nobody calls me that." Mack balled up his fist and punched Rippy on the side of his face.

"I gave her the amulet when you were just a boy. I wanted more than just friendship. She rebuked my advances."

"So, it was you that planted the bomb?"

"No. I just blackmailed someone else into doing it."

"No difference!" Mack shouted. "You are responsible!"

I'll give you a chance you didn't give me," Mack said pointing to Rippy's pistol lying on the desk.

Rippy leaned forward and inched his hand closer to the pistol. Mack lowered his weapon. At the sight of Mack lowering his pistol, Rippy made his move. Rippy grabbed the pistol and dove onto the floor. Rippy started firing the instant he hit the ground. Not flinching, Mack returned fire striking Rippy several times. As Rippy lay bleeding on the floor, Mack placed the pistol back in Dillinger's hand.

"This isn't over," Rippy managed to spit out.

"It is for you," Mack said as he placed a round into Rippy's head.

CHAPTER SEVENTEEN

Mack picked up Rippy's cell phone and put it into his pocket. He noticed an address written on a tablet on Rippy's desk. He tore the page from the tablet and walked out of the residence and back to Dillinger's van. As he dug around in the van, he discovered a slip of paper with the same address written on it. *This has got to be where they are holding Candy.*

Mack started the engine, shoved the transmission into drive and sped towards the address. His mind was racing. He had only a short time to get to Candy and rescue her. He reached down and pulled his mother's amulet from under his shirt. *I told you that they would pay with their lives.* A sense of relief rushed over Mack. Nothing could bring his mother back, but at least he got the person responsible. He could now close that chapter in his life.

Mack located the address which was only a few miles from Rippy. He pulled out the cell phone and sent a text message to Becker. *"Bring the bitch to me."* In a few minutes he received a response. *"The bitch is on her way."* Mack got out of the van and took up a position near the entrance to the house. He pulled out the pistol, screwed on the silencer, and crouched down behind the bushes.

"Get moving bitch," Becker said shoving Candy through the front door.

"Stop it. You're hurting me."

"Keep moving. Maybe we will have a little fun before we get to where we're going. It would go easier on you."

"Screw you…you bastard," Candy said as she pulled away from Becker's grasp.

"Oh, so you like it rough do you? Fine with me, the rougher the better."

"You will get what's coming to you," Candy said as she spit in Becker's face.

"And who is going to save you now, bitch?"

"Me," Mack said as he revealed himself from the bushes.

Becker moved to pull his pistol from his jacket but Mack fired a shot into Becker's right knee. He dropped to the ground screaming in pain.

"Shut up," Mack said in his Russian accent.

"I know you," Becker said. "You're the one who blew up Osterman. I recognize you from the surveillance photo. You're with the Russian mob."

"Things aren't always as they seem. Give me a good reason why I shouldn't shoot you right now?"

"I'm dead either way. You shoot me, I'm dead. If I go back without the guy who killed Osterman, I'm dead," Becker said.

"You want the guy who killed Osterman? Here's his address," Mack said pulling out a piece of paper. "He's already dead. It's your only way out now. Make up your mind."

"You're going to let me go?"

"You go back and tell your bosses that the guy that killed Osterman is dead. There's another body there that looks like me. Need I say more?"

"No. I get you completely."

"One more thing," Mack said pointing the pistol at Becker's head. "You had better be convincing or I will track you down and finish what I started."

Mack reached down and pulled the pistol out of Becker's pocket. "Wouldn't want you shooting me in the back as I walked away."

Mack took Candy by the hand and led her away from the residence. She was shaking terribly from the ordeal she just witnessed.

"You okay?" Mack asked as he opened the door to the van.

"I don't understand. You're with the Russian mob? You kill people? What is happening?" Candy asked repeatedly.

"I will answer all your questions in due course."

"Why did you let that guy go? He will come after you…after us."

"Sometimes you have to dance with the devil. He won't come after us. If he does, he has to admit that he didn't catch the guy that killed his boss. They would make an example of him. I gave him a way out and one for us too. You still want to be with me?"

"More than ever," Candy said bursting into tears.

"Good. It's all done then. Got some spending money," Mack said pointing to the garbage bag packed full of money. "How about another trip to Vegas?"

"I'll go anywhere you want," Candy said as Mack started the vehicle. Maybe Las Vegas will be as exciting as last time."

"It wouldn't surprise me a bit," Mack said with a grin and a wink.

"I'll remember to pack my white bikini." Candy said as she winked back.

www.ingramcontent.com/pod-product-compliance
Lightning Source LLC
Chambersburg PA
CBHW070922180626
46817CB00003B/1174